KU-737-885

THE HEREFORDSHIRE HANGMEN

October, 1891: When a corpse is discovered hanging from a tree in the Malvern Hills, Detective Inspector Samuel Ravenscroft and his colleague Constable Tom Crabb are called in to investigate. However, in a case full of twists and turns, with witnesses who are less than helpful if not outright deceitful, merely establishing the identity of the murdered man proves a challenge. Gradually, the detectives follow a complex and often dangerous trail that leads from the Herefordshire countryside to the Foundling Hospital of Limehouse in London, and even across the Atlantic, in a quest to bring the Herefordshire Hangmen to justice.

Books by Kerry Tombs
Published by Ulverscroft:

THE LEDBURY LAMPLIGHTERS
THE DROITWICH DECEIVERS
THE PERSHORE POISONERS

KERRY TOMBS

THE HEREFORDSHIRE HANGMEN

Complete and Unabridged

ULVERSCROFT
Leicester

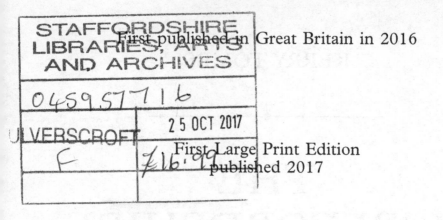

STAFFORDSHIRE
LIBRARIES, ARTS
AND ARCHIVES

0459577116

ULVERSCROFT   2 5 OCT 2017

F   £16·99

First published in Great Britain in 2016

First Large Print Edition
published 2017

The moral right of the author has been asserted

Copyright © 2016 by Kerry Tombs
All rights reserved

A catalogue record for this book is available
from the British Library.

ISBN 978–1–4448–3482–6

Published by
F. A. Thorpe (Publishing)
Anstey, Leicestershire

Set by Words & Graphics Ltd.
Anstey, Leicestershire
Printed and bound in Great Britain by
T. J. International Ltd., Padstow, Cornwall

This book is printed on acid-free paper

Contents

Prologue

Malvern Hills, October 1891

'Sorry to have called you out here at such a late hour, sir, but it isn't every day that we find a body hanging from a tree.'

'No, I suppose not, Sergeant,' said Ravenscroft, holding the lantern aloft so that he could light his way over the uneven ground. 'Who found the body?'

'Some old farm labourer out walking his dog.'

'I wonder what he was doing up here on such an inclement evening,' put in Constable Crabb, following on behind.

Ravenscroft paused to recover his breathing, and to wipe the driving rain away from his spectacles.

'I should warn you, sir, it's not a pleasant sight,' remarked the sergeant.

'I understand; death seldom is.'

'Some of the birds have had a go at him, but I thought it better if we left him where he was until you had seen him, sir.'

'Quite right, Sergeant. The poor fellow,' said Ravenscroft, bringing the lantern closer and looking up at the body. 'Evidently someone tied one end of the rope round that branch, and the other round his neck, before pulling the man off the ground.'

'Shall we take him down, sir?'

'Yes, Sergeant. I suppose that would be the kindest thing to do.'

'Here, you men, take hold of his legs whilst I climb up this tree,' instructed the policeman, addressing two uniformed officers who stood nearby.

Ravenscroft turned away from the body.

'Who the devil would want to hang a man out here at this godforsaken place?' asked a visibly shaken Crabb.

'Who indeed?' replied Ravenscroft, turning up his collar against the cold wind and driving rain that were blowing across the hill.

'Easy there, men — get ready to catch hold of him as I cut the rope,' said the sergeant, edging slowly along the branch.

'Why go to all this trouble?' continued Crabb, wishing he were still at home in front of his warm open fire.

'Who found this man?' asked Ravenscroft, turning to face the small group of onlookers.

'I did, sir,' offered an elderly man with a ruddy complexion and untidy hair, emerging from out of the darkness.

'And you are?'

'Caleb Robinson, your honour,' replied the man, removing his cap.

'When did you find the body?'

'Just after six o'clock tonight, your worship.'

'I am not your honour or worship. And what were you doing up here on top of this hill at that hour? It must have been getting quite dark by then.'

'I was taking Jasper here out for his evening walk.'

Ravenscroft looked down at the old sheepdog standing by the man's side, as the animal let out a bark of acknowledgement.

'Not the most suitable place for a walk,' suggested Constable Crabb.

'Well, we comes up here most evenings. Jasper, he just loves to run over the hills.' The old man grinned, exposing a jagged set of uneven dark-stained teeth. 'It were Jasper here who found him.'

'Did you come up here yesterday?' asked Ravenscroft.

'Yes, sir.'

'And I presume the man was not here then?'

'Course not. I would have reported it then, wouldn't I?' retorted the man, his companion growling as he focused his eyes on the detective.

Ravenscroft smiled briefly. 'Quite. And where do you live, Mr Robinson?'

'Over at Eastnor, in the cottage next to the old post office.'

'I know it well,' said Crabb.

'Rather a long way to come for an evening walk on such an inclement night,' suggested Ravenscroft.

'Not really. There's a short cut through Deer Park, and up through the woods — and it weren't raining when we left home.'

'The man was dead when you found him?'

'I suppose he were. I didn't stop to take a closer look at him, but he weren't twitching, or moaning, or anything like that,' replied the man with some degree of relish.

'So what did you do then?'

'I walked all the way down the path to the inn below on the road. They sent a lad on a horse to the station in Ledbury. We waited at the inn until your sergeant arrived.'

'You did well, Mr Robinson.'

'Easy there, lads; lower him onto the ground,' instructed the sergeant before clambering down from the tree.

'Tell me, Mr Robinson, when you and your dog were making your way up into the hills this evening, did you happen to pass by anyone else?'

'No, I don't think so,' replied the man,

scratching his head. 'But then again, maybe I did, or maybe I didn't . . . No, I don't recall seeing anyone.'

'Well did you, or did you not, pass anyone on the way up here?' persisted Ravenscroft, finding himself becoming annoyed at the man's shifting uncertainty.

'No. There was only that horse.'

'What horse?'

'A horse. I heard the sound of a horse in the wood.'

'Did you see who was riding this horse?' asked Ravenscroft eagerly.

'No. I said I only heard the sound of a horse. I never said I saw it,' said the man, becoming irritated by the detective's questions.

'Fine. Constable Crabb, let's see what we can find out about this poor fellow,' said Ravenscroft, turning away from the man and his dog and bringing the lantern closer to the body on the ground. 'Male, age probably late twenties in years, unshaven, ruddy brown complexion suggesting that he worked out of doors, generally unkempt appearance — a labourer of some kind, judging by the state of his worn clothes. There's a small scar on his left cheek. There appear to be no obvious signs of death other than by strangulation. I would think he's been here for some hours. Let me look at his hands. Some wear, but not excessively so, suggesting that although the man was from the poorer classes, he wasn't engaged in heavy manual labour. No ink stains on the fingers, so obviously he wasn't a clerk. Has anyone here seen this man before?'

'No, sir,' replied the sergeant and the two constables, almost in unison.

'Mr Robinson?'

'Stranger to me, your honour,' replied the man, as Jasper gave another bark. 'Get back there, boy.'

'Let's examine his pockets and see if we can find any clues as to his identity,' said Ravenscroft, passing over the lantern to Crabb. The group stood in silence, watching the detective as he conducted his search.

'Completely empty — no money, no papers, not even a pocket watch. There's a hole, however, in his coat pocket. I wonder if anything might have slipped through the lining . . . Ah, what's this?' said Ravenscroft, standing upright.

Crabb and the others edged forwards.

'A small round pill box. It says 'Doctor Gazzey's Wonder Pills' on the lid. That's interesting. Still three left inside. I wonder what condition he was taking these for. I suspect it's probably some kind of quack medicine. Anyway, I suggest we get out of this unpleasant weather as soon as possible. Sergeant, would you and your men load the body onto the wagon, and then take him to the morgue. We'll see if a closer examination there will provide us with any additional information.'

'Yes, sir. Right, you men take hold of his legs. Let's be quick about it. We should have all been in our beds two hours ago.'

'Thank you, Mr Robinson,' said Ravenscroft. 'You may go now. You did the right thing in informing us. We know where you are should we need to have further words with you.'

'Glad to have been of assistance,' replied the man, raising his cap once more before he and his barking dog took their leave.

'Well, Tom, I wonder what brought our man up here on such a wet windy day as this,' mused Ravenscroft as the two detectives watched the wagon and its load begin its slow journey down the hill.

'Perhaps he was killed elsewhere,' suggested Crabb.

'If that was so, why bring the body all the way up here, when it would have been easier to have left it in some ditch by the roadside? No, I think he'd arranged to meet someone in this forlorn place, and that person or persons then killed him.'

'You think there could've been more than one of them?'

'Probably. One man must have held the man upright whilst the other man pulled on the rope; although there is the possibility, I suppose, that one man could have rendered the victim senseless before placing the knot round his neck and hauling him off his feet.'

'But if they killed him first, why go to the bother of hanging him from that tree when they could've just left the corpse on the ground?'

'Yes, that is perplexing, unless of course the man was still alive when the rope was placed around his neck.'

'You mean whoever killed him gained some kind of satisfaction from watching the poor man die?' Crabb said.

'That could have been so, in which case the victim suffered a particularly unpleasant death. It may not even have been quick, and there would have been no one else out here to have come to his assistance. It doesn't bear thinking about,' said Ravenscroft, turning away as he felt a cold shiver run down his spine.

'What a way to die,' muttered an ashen-faced Crabb. 'No one deserves to go like that.'

'Robinson said he thought he heard the

sound of a horse in the wood. I wonder if its rider was our killer.'

'It could have been, sir.'

'Shame that Robinson did not see who was riding the horse. It's no good us returning tomorrow to see if we can find some tracks in the wood; this heavy rain will have washed any remaining evidence away. I wonder why our man was murdered in such a brutal fashion. Whoever killed him must have been acting out some kind of personal revenge, and was deciding to take the law into his own hands. He, or they, obviously came fully prepared, hence the rope. We must find our Tom who has committed this terrible crime, but first we have to identify our victim. We'll have some photographs taken of the poor man in the morning, and also circulate his description, as well as seeing if anyone locally has been reported as missing. This man may well have had a wife and children. He certainly had a father and mother. Someone will be missing him, and may wish to claim the body.'

'Yes, sir,' said Crabb.

'Well there's nothing more we can do out here tonight. Let's get out of this rain and wind, and return home. We've had more than our fair share of investigating crimes on these hills over the years. Good God, Crabb, I have

just realised something!' exclaimed Ravenscroft suddenly.

'What is it, sir?'

'I've just remembered the name of this hill.'

'Yes?'

'If my memory serves me correctly, we're
standing right here on — Hangman Hill!'

1

Ledbury

'Do you know, this fellow is really quite clever,' remarked Ravenscroft.

'Who is?' asked Lucy, his wife.

'Conan Doyle.'

The couple were sitting before an open fire in their cottage in Church Lane.

'Oh, you've been reading those stories again.'

'And very ingenious they are as well. I've just completed 'The Red-Headed League',' said Ravenscroft, removing his spectacles and wiping them vigorously on his handkerchief.

'What a strange title,' remarked Lucy, looking up from her needlework.

'It's all about a pawnbroker who has red hair, and who answers an advertisement for red-headed men to undertake employment with an organisation entitled the Red-Headed League. When he attends the interview he is successful in gaining the position, and every day afterwards he sits in the offices of the society, copying out pages from *The Encyclopaedia Britannica*, between the hours of ten in the morning and two in the afternoon.'

'What a strange thing to do.'

'Well, Sherlock Holmes takes up the case, and discovers that the only reason why the red-headed pawnbroker was paid to copy out these pages is so that a group of unsavoury characters can gain access to his shop premises during his absence, when they can go down into his cellar and start digging a tunnel,' continued Ravenscroft, replacing his spectacles and leaning forwards as he warmed to his narrative.

'And why were these men digging a tunnel underneath the pawnbroker's shop?' asked an intrigued Lucy.

'So that they could secure a way into the vaults of the nearby bank. But in order to do so, they had to make sure that the pawnbroker was out of the way so that they could conduct their work without being detected. Brilliant idea, is it not?'

'I suppose your Sherlock Holmes solves the crime and apprehends the perpetrators?'

'Of course; you would expect nothing else. Mr Doyle certainly has some imaginative ideas for his stories, although I think he based his detective Sherlock Holmes on a certain Auguste Dupin.'

'And who was this Auguste Dupin?'

'He was the creation of the American

writer, Edgar Allan Poe. In his story 'The Murders in the Rue Morgue', Dupin solves the mystery by deciphering certain clues that the murderer had left behind him at the scene of the crime. It was written about fifty years ago, I believe.'

'Was your Mr Doyle a policeman before he took up writing?'

'A medical practitioner, I believe; but apparently writing detective stories pays more than attending to the sick.'

'Perhaps you should take up writing, Samuel. I'm sure the public would like to know how you solved some of your greatest cases,' said Lucy, reaching for her needle-work.

'I don't think I could do that.'

'And whyever not? You could write all about those murders you've solved since you came to Ledbury, to say nothing about your earlier experiences in Whitechapel. I'm sure that if you had still been there at the time of those terrible murders, you would have caught that horrible Jack the Ripper in no time.'

'Maybe, but I was otherwise engaged in solving that crime in Worcester, and paying court to you, my dear. A far more important occupation,' said Ravenscroft with a smile. 'No, I don't think I would have the ability to put pen to paper. I don't have the patience, or the time,' he added dismissively.

'You don't know what you could do until you try. As for the time, you're always complaining that you're bored because nothing happens in Ledbury for weeks on end.'

'Perhaps when I retire.'

'I'm sure people will be most intrigued to learn how you arrived at your clever deductions. Look at the many criminals you've put behind bars.'

'I suppose there must be quite a number, although some of them were hung; but the problem is that a number of other people who were involved in the cases are still alive and might not like what I decide to write. It would all then become a question of confidentiality.'

'You could always change the names of the people, and even some of the details. Who's not to know that one day the exploits of Samuel Ravenscroft may even come to rival those of the great Sherlock Holmes?'

'I don't think so. Anyway, Sherlock Holmes isn't a real person, whereas I am.'

'Now I think you're just making excuses.'

'We'll see,' said Ravenscroft, retreating behind his magazine and feeling that he was being backed into a corner.

'Have you had any further news about that

poor man you found on the hill?' asked Lucy, changing the subject.

'I'm afraid not. It's been almost three weeks since we found his body, and despite issuing a description of the man to all the local newspapers, no one has yet come forward to identify him.'

'Perhaps he was a stranger to these parts.'

'I think you may be correct. It's very frustrating. All we found on him was that small box of pills. They were evidently some kind of quack medicine, for I can find no details of 'Doctor Gazzey's Wonder Pills' mentioned in any of the medical books. No, unless something happens quite soon, I fear we will be forced to abandon the case, although I would be loath to do that. I'd still like to feel that we could secure some kind of justice for the victim by bringing his murderers to account.'

'What a terrible crime. I can't imagine the agony he must have gone through. I feel sure that something will happen quite soon.'

'I wished I shared your optimism, my dear. Let me see, what time is it?' asked Ravenscroft, taking out his pocket watch. 'Twenty minutes past eight. I said I'd meet Tom at the Mop Fair at around this time to see how things are proceeding. We're not expecting any trouble, as people are generally good-natured at these things, but you never know. I hope you will excuse me. I shouldn't be gone for too long.'

'Samuel, I wonder if I might accompany you? I should so like to see the fair,' asked Lucy, laying down her sewing.

'Of course you shall, my dear. I'll be glad of the company.'

★ ★ ★

'Good evening to you, Mrs Ravenscroft,' said the young fresh-faced constable.

'Good evening to you, Tom,' replied Lucy. 'I haven't seen you recently. I trust Jennie and the children are well?'

'Very well, Mrs Ravenscroft, although the young one do keep us awake at night.'

'I know,' said Lucy with a smile.

'And how are things here, Tom?' asked Ravenscroft, looking across the marketplace towards the streets full of crowded people.

'No problems, sir. Everyone seems quite happy. Some of the Leewood lads are in a boisterous mood, but I've had a word with them, and I've got the men at the ready should any trouble break out.'

'Let's hope they won't be needed. There are certainly a great many people here tonight. Shall we go and see what entertainment is on offer?' asked Ravenscroft, linking his wife's arm. 'I'll see you later, Tom.'

'Yes, sir. Mrs Ravenscroft.'

The detective and Lucy made their way through the noisy crowds of people that flocked along the Homend, pausing now and then to look at the varied entertainment that was on offer from the numerous stalls and booths. A juggler was receiving applause as a group of musicians wandered up and down the street, and a number of children called out excitedly from a revolving carousel.

'Pretty ribbons for the lady,' said an old woman presenting up her wares for Lucy to inspect.

'How much is the red one?' asked Lucy.

'Two pence, my lovely,' replied the woman.

'Could I have it, Samuel? It would go so well with my bonnet.'

'Of course, my dear,' replied Ravenscroft, handing over a coin to the woman.

'Bless you both, and may good fortune go with you.'

Ravenscroft and Lucy continued on their way along the street.

'Now then, which of you Ledbury lads will be brave enough to step up here and take on the Mighty Goliath? Five pounds to anyone who can last two rounds with him,' shouted a bald fat man dressed in a blood-stained shirt and trousers as he gestured towards a scrawny ugly-looking man who was making wild jabbing movements into the air.

'You must be having us on!' replied one of the young men from the crowd of laughing onlookers. 'He looks as though he wouldn't last five seconds!'

'Then you will be taking him, on sir? How about you as well, sir? Who else wants to try his luck? Step this way, folks, and enter the tent — only three pence to see the bout!'

'Go on, Daniel, see if you can slay the brute!' shouted out a voice.

'Let's see what we can find further down the street,' suggested Ravenscroft, guiding Lucy away from the excited crowd.

'Step inside now, ladies and gentlemen. Only tuppence to see Florinda the famous Bearded Lady, and Gerome the Italian Midget Extraordinaire!' urged a tall showman who was smiling as he waved a large red hat in the air.

'Do you wish to see these curiosities, my dear?' laughed Ravenscroft.

'I certainly do not.'

'Let's see what that fellow is all about over there. He seems to have attracted quite a large crowd,' said Ravenscroft, moving across to where a tall bearded man wearing a striped suit and sporting a bright canary-coloured waistcoat and stovepipe hat was issuing forth.

'Good evening, ladies and gentlemen! May

I introduce myself to you good noble citizens of Ledbury. My name is Silas Lincoln Rockstone, and as you can tell from the colour of my apparel and the tone of my voice, I am not from these parts. No, sir. I hail from the great city of New York! And you may well be thinking, what's a fine upstanding gentleman like me doing here tonight? Well I can tell you, my good people of Ledbury, that I am on a mission. Oh yes, sir, I am on a mission to save you all!'

'Come on, my dear. I think we've heard enough of this nonsense,' said Ravenscroft, turning away from the showman. 'I'm not in the mood tonight for any kind of religious conversion.'

'I think he's quite entertaining. Oh Samuel, do let us stay and see what he has to say,' implored Lucy.

'If you really must insist.'

'I have come here tonight not to save your souls, but your bodies!' continued the showman with a dramatic flourish. 'I have heard that the inhabitants of this quaint old English town do not require God. No, sir! They are religious enough! I have come here amongst you tonight to cure your ailments and ills. I've heard that this is a sick town. Oh yes! There are people hereabouts who are lying in their beds suffering from all kinds of illnesses, coughing and sweating, unable to do a day's honest work without enduring unspeakable agonies. There are young men and women amongst you here tonight who are old before their time. Many of you have numerous aches and pains, being afflicted by weakened bones, whilst others of you have ugly warts and other unsightly marks that will not disappear.

'Last month I was in New York when I had a dream. Yes, my friends, a dream. And in my dream a voice called out to me, 'Save the good folks of Ledbury. They are a crying out for relief from their suffering. You must travel across the mighty Atlantic Ocean and help the afflicted.' Well, I tell you that help is now at hand to save you, my brothers and sisters. Do not despair, as I have come amongst you to cure you all! I have cured the sick and the infirm of New York City, and now I am here amongst you tonight to offer you the divine intervention of Silas Lincoln Rockstone! I have a large bag here that contains all my secret medical remedies. You tell me your complaint, and I guarantee that I'll have something here that will cure it. Who will be the first to step forward and ask to be cured?'

A silence fell upon the audience.

'Come now; don't be shy. Who will be bold enough step forward?'

'I will,' shouted out a youth from the back of the crowd.

'Who calls? Don't be shy. Come forward, young man, and show yourself,' urged the showman.

The crowd parted as the youth came closer towards the small platform upon which the speaker stood.

'Have I not seen you before, young man?'

'Yes, sir; last week in Bromsgrove.'

'Ah yes, I remember. And what was your complaint, my young man?'

'Me face, sir; it were all covered in boils, sir. Nasty boils; big red horrible boils. They used to itch and burst wide open!' replied the youth with dramatic effect, as several members of the audience exclaimed.

'And how many of these boils were there?' asked the showman intently.

'Ten, sir,' replied the youth somewhat hesitantly.

'Ten boils! But I can see no boils now. Where are your boils?' asked the man, looking down seriously at the youth.

'All gone, sir.'

'All gone! And why have these boils gone?'

'Because of the ointment, sir.'

'Ah, the ointment — and from whom did you acquire this miraculous medication?'

'Why, from you, sir.'

'Was this the ointment?' asked Rockstone, reaching into a large black bag that had been positioned on a stool at his side and bringing forth a small green jar, as some members of the audience gasped.

'Yes, sir.'

'So you purchased this ointment from me but seven days ago, and you followed my instructions?'

'Yes, sir. I rubbed the cream on my face twice a day as you said, sir.'

'Step up here, my good man,' instructed Rockstone. 'Let me look at your face. I can see no boils. Now turn to my friends; let them gaze upon you. Can any of you see any boils on this man's face?'

There was loud muttering in the audience as the throng began to edge forwards.

'Now I will give a shiny sixpence to anyone here tonight who can see a boil on this man's face,' challenged the showman, peering at his audience through his large spectacles.

Again the crowd moved even closer to the platform.

'I'm cured!' shouted the young man, flinging his arms so wildly into the air that the front row of the crowd recoiled.

'Do you hear that, my friends? This man has been cured in only seven days!' shouted Rockstone triumphantly, brandishing the youth's arm. 'And how much did you pay, sir, for this miracle?'

'Three pence, sir.'

'Only three pence! A small price to pay for such a miracle! Thank you, my good man. You may now step down. Now which of you here would care to purchase a bottle of my preparation? Not only will it banish boils forever, but it will also remove spots, warts and smallpox scars, even unsightly birthmarks. Apply twice a day to the disfigured area, and I can guarantee that within a week your affflictions will be a thing of the past. Thank you kindly, sir. Thank you, madam. You will not regret your investment, I can assure you. Thank you. Thank you.'

'What nonsense,' said Ravenscroft to his wife as they watched the showman handing over his jars of ointment to eager members of his audience.

'Can't you arrest him?' asked Lucy. 'The man is clearly making false claims for his miracle cream.'

'What for? If the fools want to part with their money, who am I to prevent them?'

'Thank you folks most kindly. Now what else can I help you with? Aching backs? Noisy coughs? Dizzy spells? I have just the thing here,' continued the American.

'I would like some of Doctor Gazzey's Wonder Pills,' shouted out Ravenscroft from the back of the crowd.

23

The showman paused for a moment as he peered into the audience, trying to ascertain who had asked the question.

'Do you have any of Doctor Gazzey's Wonder Pills?' repeated Ravenscroft.

'Who asks?' enquired a hesitant Rockstone.

'A friend of mine has recently taken some of Doctor Gazzey's pills,' continued Ravenscroft as a hush descended on the audience. 'I wondered whether you had some for me to purchase?'

'I do indeed, my good sir,' said the showman, reaching once more into his bag. 'I think this is what you're looking for, sir. Guaranteed to cure all ills and revive the tired constitution, as well as putting a smile on your good lady's face.'

Lucy blushed as several members of the crowd laughed.

'I would seek a quiet word with you, sir,' requested Ravenscroft, moving closer to the platform.

'The gentleman requires a quiet word with me. I wonder what that can be about!' exclaimed Rockstone as more laughter broke out in the audience. 'We can't keep the lady waiting, can we?'

'A word with you, sir; I am a police officer,' said Ravenscroft, leaning forward and whispering into the man's ear.

'Right. I see. Okay, folks, that's all for now,' replied a shaken Rockstone, to loud groans from the audience.

'Perhaps we could go somewhere more private?' suggested Ravenscroft.

'If you and your good lady would care to follow me into the tent over there, I'm sure we won't be disturbed,' said the American, quickly recovering his composure.

Ravenscroft and Lucy followed the man across the street and into the small bell tent that had been erected in front of one of the buildings.

'Now, my good sir, before you seek to question me about my remedies, I can assure you that I am a graduate of the finest university in New York City, and that I can produce a long list of patients who can vouch for the effectiveness of my cures. Why, you saw now how that youth has been saved from his terrible affliction. You'll find nothing wrong with my medicines and ointments,' declared the man, speaking in a quick manner before Ravenscroft could utter a word.

'Did I do all right, Mr Rockstone?' asked a voice as someone suddenly parted the flaps of the tent. Ravenscroft recognised the youth who had spoken up at the gathering.

'Go away! Can't you see I'm busy?' growled the showman.

'An acquaintance of yours?' said Ravenscroft, smiling.

'Now then, my good sir, I can see that you're a man of this world. You have no doubt purchased such medicines in the past, and can see that they cause no harm,' said a smiling Rockstone, placing his hand on Ravenscroft's shoulder.

'That's a matter for debate, sir. All I can see is that you're a charlatan seeking to separate the good citizens of Ledbury from their hard-earned savings.'

'Come now, I seek to deceive no one. My cures have been tested on many people with great success. Why, there are thousands in New York City who have given thanks for the better lives they're leading today, all because they took one or more of my medicines. Why, even the president of the United States and his good wife have benefitted from my expertise. You'd surely not deprive the good folks of Ledbury from receiving the care and attention that they need?' said Rockstone in his defence.

'It is a wicked act, sir, to deprive honest people of their savings,' declared an indignant Lucy.

'You have proof of that accusation, my dear lady?'

'I haven't come here tonight to enquire into

the medicinal properties of your so-called cures,' said Ravenscroft. 'All I seek from you is some information.'

'Information?'

'Yes. I presume that Doctor Gazzey's Wonder Pills are one of your creations?'

'They are indeed, and proud I am of them.'

'Have you sold many boxes of these pills recently?'

'Not for several weeks. I'm waiting for a new supply to be shipped over from New York.'

'Why would I wish to purchase such an item? What ailment would you seek to cure me of with it?' enquired Ravenscroft.

'Whatever concerns you at the present time, sir. Fatigue, aching bones, laxity, increased circulation, general wellbeing,' replied Rock-stone proudly.

'I must confide in you, sir,' said Ravenscroft, drawing nearer. 'I am at present investigating a murder.'

'A murder!'

'Yes, and a rather unpleasant one at that. Just over two weeks ago a man was found hanging from one of the trees in the Malvern Hills. Despite extensive police enquiries, we have been unable to identify the victim, but inside the man's pocket we found a small box containing your pills.'

'I see. And you are Sergeant — ?'

'I am Inspector Ravenscroft of the local constabulary.'

'Inspector Ravenscroft,' repeated an uneasy Rockstone. 'Pray, Inspector, would you be able to describe this unfortunate man?'

'I can indeed, Mr Rockstone. He was aged around thirty, with a dark brown appearance, and probably of the labouring classes, although his hands were not excessively worn. He had a small scar on his left cheek.'

'Oh my lord!' exclaimed the doctor, bringing his hand up to his forehead.

'You know the gentleman?' asked Ravenscroft hopefully.

'Indeed I do. The man is Jacob. Poor Jacob!'

'Jacob, you say? I presume that was his Christian name? You have a last name, sir?'

'No, no, we knew him only as Jacob.'

'When did you last see this man?'

'About three weeks ago. The fair was in Hereford at the time. He just left one night without any warning. He just left.'

'Was this man employed by you, or by the fair?'

'Both.'

'What kind of work was he engaged in?'

'He helped generally with the fair, assisting with the setting up and taking down of the various tents and booths, advertising the fair in towns before our arrival, driving the wagons, helping run the stalls, that kind of thing. The reason he may have had the box of pills in his pocket was because he would often produce them when I . . . er, addressed the crowds,' stuttered Rockstone.

'You mean that he was usually the person in the audience who claimed he'd been cured?' said Ravenscroft, smiling.

'I find that members of the public are somewhat reticent in coming forward. If they can see, however, that one of their number has been cured, they're more inclined to step forward. It is all quite legal, my dear Inspector. Merely a little mild entertainment. It does no harm.'

'How long had this Jacob been in the fair's employment?'

'Nearly two years.'

'Where did you first meet him?'

'In New York City.'

'So he was American?' asked Lucy.

'Oh no, my good lady; he was English.'

'And what was an Englishman doing in New York?' asked Ravenscroft, anxious to know more about the unfortunate man.

'I have no idea. He never said. I remember he just came to the fair one day and enquired if he could seek employment with us.'

'Tell me, Mr Rockstone, when did the fair

leave New York and come to England?'

'About six months ago.'

'Was Jacob happy to be returning to the country of his birth?'

'If he was, he didn't show it. He seemed quite indifferent.'

'When you and your colleagues came to England, which part of the country did you travel to?'

'Rather a strange question, Inspector.'

'Nevertheless, I'd be grateful if you could answer it.'

'The fair first travelled around the villages near London, then upwards towards your Manchester and then across to your north Wales.'

'And during these travels, did Jacob ever speak about where he might have originated from?'

'No, I believe not,' answered the puzzled showman. 'But I do remember that just before we moved down to Hereford, he became very upset, saying that he believed the fair would do no good there, and that we should go further into south Wales instead.'

'That is all very interesting. But you say that the fair did go to Hereford, and that was when he left suddenly?'

'That's correct, Inspector. I remember I was addressing a large crowd there, and was waiting for Jacob to cry out from the audience, but he never appeared. It was all most unsettling.'

'During all the time you knew Jacob, he never told you his last name, nor spoke of his former life in this country?' asked Ravenscroft, deep in thought.

'That was indeed so, Inspector.'

'Did you not find that strange?'

'Some people are like that. They want to forget the past. In my profession we learn not to ask too many questions.'

'Quite. Thank you, Mr Rockstone. Just one more question. When Jacob left, did he take any of his personal effects with him?'

'No; that was the strange thing. He left all his belongings behind. It was almost as though something frightened him, and he wanted to get away in a hurry.'

'I wonder whether you still have any of those personal items?'

'I'm afraid not. There was nothing of any value; just a few old clothes. We discarded those after a few days when the fair moved on, and when it seemed that he wasn't going to return.'

'There were no letters, books, inscribed watches, anything like that?'

'No, there was nothing of that nature.'

'You're certain on that point?'

'Of course,' replied Rockstone, turning away.

'I have to tell you, sir, that I don't believe you. I find it extraordinary that a man can disappear without any kind of warning, leaving his possessions behind him, and yet you say you found nothing of a personal nature,' said Ravenscroft, speaking directly to the showman.

'I've told you I have nothing that belonged to Jacob,' protested Rockstone.

'And I tell you that I believe you're lying to us. If I call out now, Mr Rockstone, I can summon three policemen into this tent, and not only will we make a thorough search of your person and your effects, but we will also make sure that the fair is closed down immediately, and that you and your colleagues are driven out of the three counties. I trust I make my intentions clear on that point?'

'You do indeed, Inspector. There was this,' said Rockstone, reluctantly reaching into his coat pocket. 'I was of course keeping it in case Jacob returned.'

'Thank you, Mr Rockstone,' said Ravenscroft, accepting a small silver locket and chain which the showman placed in his hand. 'It would have saved us all a great deal of trouble if you'd given this to me earlier in our conversation. Let's see what is inside ... A miniature of a young woman. What do you make of it, my dear?'

'What an exquisite picture,' said Lucy, after taking the locket from her husband. 'And the subject is certainly a beauty. Her name appears to be Maria, according to the writing opposite.'

'Did Jacob ever speak of this item, or of the lady depicted?' asked Ravenscroft.

'No. I only found the item when I was clearing out his effects.'

'I shall need to take possession of the locket whilst we make further investigations,' said the detective.

'Of course, Inspector; I understand. Now we know that Jacob will unfortunately not be returning, I can no longer justify retaining the item.'

'Before we leave, Mr Rockstone, I'd be obliged if you would tell me your future movements, in case I need to contact you again.'

'Yes, Inspector. We have two more nights here, then the fair travels next to your Tewkesbury, where we'll be until the end of the week. Next week I believe we'll be going on to the town of Evesham, and then we go to Chipping Norton.'

'Thank you, Mr Rockstone. May I give you

my card? Should you remember anything further concerning Jacob, I'd be grateful if you would contact me,' instructed Ravenscroft as he and Lucy began to leave.

'Certainly, Inspector. I'll make enquiries of the other fair-people to see if Jacob confided in them.'

'I am much obliged to you.'

'Jacob may have had a rather reserved nature, but he was a pleasant enough fellow. I hope that you're successful in apprehending his killer.'

'I can assure you, Mr Rockstone, that'll we endeavour to do all that we can to obtain justice for the fellow,' said Ravenscroft as he and Lucy took their leave.

2

Ledbury and Cirencester

'Well, Tom, what do you think of that?'

Ravenscroft had just recounted the events of the previous evening, as he and Tom Crabb sat in the Ledbury Police Station early the following morning.

'That Rockstone fellow sounds like quite a charlatan. Do you think he was telling you the truth about this man Jacob?'

'I'm not sure. He was certainly reluctant to admit that he was in possession of this locket. I have no doubt he would have sold or pawned it after a suitable time had elapsed, possibly when he had returned to America. The man makes his living from selling quack potions and ointments, and promises his unfortunate victims that they will be cured of all their ills. By the time they discover that their miracle cure is nothing of the sort, Rockstone and his companions have moved on to some other location. Rockstone said that Jacob was his stooge in the audience, and that his job was to produce Gazzey's Wonder Pills, or some other fake medicine, at the appropriate moment, and then claim that he had been cured. However, when the fair was at Hereford, Jacob didn't perform his role that evening. Something or someone must have frightened him so much that he fled as quickly as he could, not even pausing to pick up his possessions.'

'He could have been kidnapped by the same people who later decided to hang him from that tree on Hangman's Hill,' suggested Crabb.

'You could be correct, but either way we know that Jacob didn't want the fair to come to Hereford, which means that he was afraid of something happening to him there. So he must have previously lived in the area, did someone a great wrong, and fled as a consequence, eventually turning up in New York some years later.'

'And the lady, sir?'

'You mean this Maria, the subject depicted inside the locket? She obviously meant a lot to Jacob, as he had retained it.'

'Perhaps the lady was his former sweetheart.'

'Or another member of his family; a sister perhaps, or even his mother. She is certainly an attractive woman, quite a beauty, although you'd better not tell Mrs Ravenscroft that I just said so. I wonder who she was, and when the portrait was executed. There's no way of telling, but it is certainly a fine piece of work. Unfortunately we're no further forward to finding out who this Jacob really was, or where he came from.'

'Rockstone could have been making the whole thing up. He could have killed Jacob.'

'Yes, there is that possibility; but if that were the case, why would he have gone to all the trouble of travelling out to Hangman Hill, and killing his victim there, when he could have just as easily drowned the body in the river at Hereford? It's almost as though Jacob had to be hung on Hangman Hill, rather than anywhere else. Whatever the man's past, that place had a special significance for his killer or killers.'

'What next then, sir?' asked Crabb.

'I don't know, Tom,' said Ravenscroft, staring at the portrait in the locket. 'If only we could identify the lady. Give me your pocket knife. It appears as though this miniature has been mounted inside the case since the time it was painted. I wonder, if I tried to lift the portrait from its setting in the locket, whether we might find something on the back.'

Crabb handed over his knife and Ravenscroft gently placed the blade at the edge of the portrait. 'There. Now let's see. There's a small rather faded signature at the bottom, on the reverse. Give me the magnifying glass. I can just make out a name. 'Louis Thermaine'.'

'He sounds French to me.'

'It is probably the name of the artist. I wonder . . . If we can find out more about this Thermaine, we might then be able to identify the young lady in the portrait, and that in turn may enable us to find out more about our victim,' said Ravenscroft, replacing the portrait back inside the locket.

'How would we do that, sir?'

'I'm not sure. Yes — of course! Come on, Tom. I think I know just the man who may be able to help us,' said Ravenscroft, eagerly rising from his chair.

★　★　★

Thirty minutes later, the two policemen found themselves standing outside a large building situated at the end of Belle Vue Terrace, in the nearby town of Great Malvern.

'I think Mr Clifford, the proprietor of the Malvern Library and Reading Rooms, may prove of assistance to us,' said Ravenscroft, pushing open the door.

'Good morning to you, sir. Why, it is Mr Ravenscroft, if I am not mistaken,' said the immaculately dressed gentleman who was standing behind a large oak counter.

'Mr Clifford; it's good to make your acquaintance again,' said Ravenscroft with a smile as he removed his hat.

'And you, Constable Crabb.'

'Good morning to you, Mr Clifford,' replied the constable.

'I trust you are both well, gentlemen?' enquired Clifford.

'Indeed so,' answered Ravenscroft.

'It's been some years since you last visited my establishment.'

'Five years, I believe,' offered Ravenscroft.

'As long as that? At the time of all those terrible murders that were taking place in Malvern, if I am not mistaken.'

'Yes, you are correct. You were able then to assist us in our enquiries. We now find ourselves requiring your assistance once again, if you'd be so kind, Mr Clifford.'

'I would be delighted, gentlemen. How may I be of help?'

'We're seeking information concerning a certain Louis Thermaine.'

'Louis Thermaine. Thermaine, you say? The name is not familiar to me. I don't believe that he could be a resident of the town, or I would have heard of the said gentleman.'

'He was an artist,' said Crabb.

'I wonder whether you have any books in your collection that might provide information regarding such a profession? In particular, he painted miniatures,' said Ravenscroft.

'What period did this artist flourish? Was he an Elizabethan or medieval artist?' asked Clifford, turning round and running his finger along one of the shelves of books on the wall.

'I don't think he was alive then. He was painting some twenty or thirty years ago. We don't know whether he's still alive today.'

'Then I don't think I can be of assistance to you, gentlemen. All my reference works contain information concerning earlier artists. I don't believe there's any current reference work that contains information regarding current artists. Now had your man been a member of the aristocracy, I'm sure we would have found him in either *Who's Who* or *Burke's Peerage*.'

'I see,' replied a somewhat disappointed Ravenscroft.

'However, all may not be lost, Inspector. There are the county volumes of *The Post Office Directory*, which may be of assistance to you. Should your gentleman still be in the land of the living, he could well be listed in one of those volumes. If you'd care to follow me, gentlemen,' said Clifford, leading the way into an inner room. 'Now would you happen to know in which part of the country your Mr Thermaine might be residing?'

'I'm afraid not,' answered Ravenscroft.

'Then there's nothing else for it; you will have to go through each county volume in turn,' said Clifford, taking down some of the books and handing one each to the two detectives. 'I suggest that you look under both Artists and also in the Court Section.'

'Thank you, Mr Clifford,' said Ravenscroft, seating himself at one of the tables. 'At least our man has a somewhat unusual name.'

'That will certainly be of great help to you. Now if you'll excuse me, I must attend to the gentleman and lady who have just entered the building,' said Clifford.

'Thank you, Mr Clifford. You've been most helpful,' said Ravenscroft as the librarian left the room.

Several minutes of silence elapsed as the two men turned over the pages of a number of the volumes.

'We don't appear to be having much success,' said a frustrated Ravenscroft. 'That was the last volume in the series.'

'Ah, I believe I may have found the gentleman!' exclaimed Crabb suddenly.

Ravenscroft stood up and looked eagerly

over his constable's shoulder. 'Well done, Tom. Louis Thermaine is listed as a resident of Cecily Hill in the Gloucestershire market town of Cirencester,' he said, adjusting his spectacles to obtain a better view of the writing. 'I wonder if he's also listed under Artists.'

'It would appear not, sir,' replied Crabb after he had examined the relevant section.

'Perhaps he no longer practises as an artist. In the absence of anyone else of the same name, I believe it's worth following up this line of enquiry. As this is the only information we've uncovered in this case, I will have to journey over to Cirencester and see if I can pay this gentleman a visit. If he's still alive, then he may be able to name the subject in the locket, and she in turn might be able to tell us more about the man Jacob.'

'What would you like me to do whilst you are away, sir?' asked Crabb.

'Go and interview as many of the fair-folk as you can. See if anyone can tell us more about Jacob. He must have confided in someone.'

'Yes, sir.'

'Now there's just one more volume I need to consult,' said Ravenscroft, looking at the books on the shelves. 'Yes, here we are — *Bradshaw's*. I can't think that there's a direct train route from Great Malvern to Cirencester. Yes, just as I thought — change trains at Worcester and Gloucester. These journeys are never easy.'

★ ★ ★

Later that morning, Ravenscroft stood in the wide-open marketplace of the Gloucestershire town of Cirencester, admiring the ancient church with its tall steeple and ornate carvings round its main entrance. He had just visited the local police station, where the officer on duty had informed him that the man he sought was still a resident of the town.

Following the directions he had been given, Ravenscroft made his way along the narrow streets before turning into a wide avenue, where a collection of fine honey-coloured houses stood on either side of the dusty road, and the entrance to a large park could be glimpsed in the distance. Arriving at one of the houses in the middle of the avenue, he tugged on the bell pull and was rewarded by the opening of the door by a middle-aged woman dressed in servant's attire.

'Good morning. I would like to speak with Monsieur Thermaine,' said Ravenscroft, smiling at the maid as he removed his hat.

'Do you have an appointment, sir?'

43

'No, but it is essential that I speak with Monsieur Thermaine,' began Ravenscroft.

'Then I'm afraid you can't see the master. He'll only see people by appointment,' replied the sour-faced maid, beginning to close the door.

'I have come upon most urgent business,' interjected Ravenscroft, placing his hand on the woodwork. 'Police business. If you would give my card to your master, I'd be obliged, and tell him that I only require a few minutes of his time.'

The maid took the card and studied it for several seconds.

'It really is most urgent,' stressed Ravenscroft.

'I'll see what the master has to say. Wait there,' snapped the unsmiling maid, quickly closing the door in Ravenscroft's face.

The inspector took out his pocket watch, then looked casually around at the other buildings in the street and up at the heavily curtained windows of the artist's residence, before walking impatiently up and down the pavement. As he found the seconds turning into minutes, and the door firmly closed in front of him, he found himself becoming more and more anxious. To have come so far, with only the most tentative of possibilities open to him, and to be denied entry at this time, was an outcome that was not to be borne.

After a further two minutes had elapsed, Ravenscroft reached out for the bell pull once more, just as the door suddenly opened before him.

'Master will see you now, but only for a few minutes.'

'Thank you. I'm much obliged,' replied a somewhat relieved Ravenscroft, stepping into the hallway.

'Follow me,' instructed the maid in a tone which Ravenscroft did not consider entirely hospitable.

The maid tapped loudly on one of the doors at the end of a badly lit passageway that Ravenscroft observed was lined with paintings. 'Enter,' cried out a cracked voice from within.

Ravenscroft found himself stepping into a small, darkened, almost airless room, where the only light seemed to come from the hearth and a solitary candle.

''Ravenscroft', it says here,' said a frail voice.

'Yes. I trust I have the honour of addressing Monsieur Louis Thermaine, the distinguished artist?' said Ravenscroft as he edged tentatively towards a small heavily wrinkled old man who was seated in an armchair situated before an almost burnt-out fire.

'You had better sit down there,' indicated the man, pointing with a long, thin, bony finger towards a wooden chair.

'Thank you, sir. I will endeavour not to take up too much of your time,' said Ravenscroft, accepting the seat.

'I can give you five minutes,' grumbled the man, causing Ravenscroft to wonder why the man's time was important to him when he had not appeared to have been engaged in any fruitful activity when he had entered the room.

'I would be grateful, sir, if you'd look at this locket for me,' said Ravenscroft, taking the item from out of his coat pocket.

The old man stared at him for several seconds before reaching out to accept the item. 'Give me that candle on the table there.'

Ravenscroft turned around, picked up the candlestick and passed it over to the old man, who accepted it with an unsteady hand. As the flickering flame drew nearer to the artist's face, Ravenscroft observed the thin paper-like skin, yellow complexion and haunted look in his eyes.

'You came by train?'

'Indeed.'

The man coughed but said nothing as Ravenscroft cast his eyes around the room.

Two or three items of mediocre continental porcelain stood at either end of the mantel over the fireplace. A faded photograph in a damaged frame assumed a lonely role on the opposite wall, and a ragged stuffed owl looked out at him from beneath a glass dome on an adjoining table. He wondered why the artist had chosen to furnish his room with such unappealing items.

Thermaine coughed again but said nothing. Ravenscroft found the long silence unsettling as the old man studied the locket intently.

'I've never seen this before. I don't know why you've come here today.'

'If you would care to open the locket, I believe you may discover something of interest,' urged Ravenscroft as the man sought to return the item.

Thermaine stared at Ravenscroft again for several seconds; then, turning his attention towards the locket, opened the cover to the case. 'Where did you get this?'

'I am making enquiries concerning the death of a man in the Malvern Hills three weeks ago. He went by the Christian name of Jacob. The locket was one of his possessions.'

'This is of no interest to me,' retorted the man, suddenly snapping the lid shut and turning away to face the dying embers in the fireplace.

'I've come here today because your name appears on the reverse of the miniature. I believe you may have painted this portrait. The sitter would appear to be called Maria,' continued Ravenscroft, finding himself somewhat at a loss due to the man's unhelpful attitude.

'I cannot help you. You'd better go,' said Thermaine.

'Then you're not the artist of this work?'

'Why do you want to know that for? It's a long time since I was engaged in such activity. I have no interest in painting now.'

'Jacob was murdered in a brutal fashion. We know nothing about him except for the fact that this locket appears to have been his most prized possession. If I am to apprehend his killer, I must know more about this man. I ask you again, sir, to take another look at this miniature and tell me what you know about the lady,' urged Ravenscroft anxiously.

'I haven't undertaken any commissions for the past fifteen years. My eyes, they are not what they were,' muttered Thermaine.

'I wonder whether you used to live in Paris?' asked Ravenscroft, realising that he would have to change the subject if he were to obtain any useful information from the artist.

'Who told you that?'

'You're French, so I assumed that you may

have once resided there.'

'The Commune!' exclaimed Thermaine, suddenly sitting upright and staring at Ravenscroft in a wild fashion.

'The Paris Commune. 1870. I remember reading about it at the time,' replied Ravenscroft, taken aback by the sudden change in the man's manner and wondering what he should say.

'They killed my friends, you know. I went back to save them, but I was too late,' said the artist as tears began to form in his eyes.

'It must have been terrible for you,' said Ravenscroft sympathetically after a moment's silence had elapsed.

'They murdered the women and children,' continued Thermaine sadly. 'Why did they do that? Will you tell me why? You have no comprehension of the situation we found ourselves in. My poor wife, they showed her no mercy.'

'I'm sorry, but you said you went back to Paris. Were you living in England before you returned to Paris?' asked Ravenscroft.

'Yes, but what is it to you?'

'That must have been difficult — I mean, finding yourself in a foreign country.'

The artist said nothing as he slumped back into his chair.

'When did you first arrive in England?'

'In 1860.'

'Where did you first go to when you came to England? London?'

'There was nothing for me there. I went to Bristol for a while, then Hereford, before coming here to Cirencester.'

'You mentioned Hereford,' said Ravenscroft eagerly. 'How long were you in Hereford?'

'I was there only for a few months. There was little work for me to undertake. The people there were all philistines. Philistines, I tell you.'

'You undertook commissions whilst in Hereford?'

'Enough!' exclaimed Thermaine, almost throwing the locket into Ravenscroft's lap before drawing a large shawl around his shoulders. 'I have answered enough of your silly questions. I want you to go now. I am tired.'

'And you can tell me nothing regarding the lady depicted in the portrait?' asked Ravenscroft, replacing the locket in his coat pocket as he stood up.

The old man said nothing, gesturing with his arm that Ravenscroft should leave, before blowing out the candle.

'It is most important that I know her name.'

Thermaine remained silent, his eyes staring into the dying embers before him.

Ravenscroft paused for a few seconds, hoping that Thermaine would say more, but eventually realising that he could obtain no further information from the artist made his way out of the room, where he found the maid waiting to escort him to the front entrance of the building.

'How long has it been since your master gave up painting?' he asked, straining to see the many portraits that adorned the walls of the dimly lit passageway.

'Master doesn't paint anymore. What business is it of yours?' muttered the servant.

'These are fine portraits. This one in particular is most interesting,' said Ravenscroft, intently studying the portrait that hung nearest the outer door.

'You should go. Master isn't well. He's not long for this world. You shouldn't come again. He doesn't like to be bothered.'

Ravenscroft took out the locket from his pocket and looked down at the miniature before casting a final glance at the portrait on the wall. 'Thank you,' he said with a smile before stepping out into the street. 'I believe I may now have all the information I need.'

3

The Verzons

'Maria Constantine!' proclaimed Ravenscroft after he had narrated the morning's events to Crabb back in Ledbury.

'Forgive me, sir, but I thought you said that Thermaine denied all knowledge of having painted the miniature?' asked a puzzled Crabb.

'He did, but it seems that he not only painted miniatures, but also made larger versions of his work. They were all hanging in his entrance hall, and one of them I recognised as the lady in the locket. Fortunately a small label at the bottom of the portrait bore the name 'Maria Constantine'.

'That was most fortunate.'

'Indeed, Tom. I can't make up my mind whether Thermaine recognised the painting in the locket and for some reason didn't want me to know who she was, or whether his mind genuinely had no recollection of the event. Either way, I suppose it doesn't matter. As you say, it was indeed fortunate that I saw the larger portrait.'

'What I find strange, sir,' remarked Crabb, 'is if Thermaine came to this county in 1860, why did he then go back to Paris in 1870, when the city was in a state of civil war?'

'Yes, I must say I do find that rather extraordinary. I wish he'd told me more about those troubled times. He did say his wife had been killed during the Commune. I wonder if she'd been left behind when Thermaine came over here in 1860, and he then returned ten years later to try and save her.'

'It seems rather strange to me to leave one's wife in one country whilst you go to another, and then you go back ten years later. I know that Mrs Crabb would never entertain such an idea.'

'Nor Mrs Ravenscroft, either. No, I feel there's another mystery waiting to be unravelled there, but I'm not sure that the solving of it would assist us in finding out more about the man we found hanging on Hangman Hill. The whole thing could have been mere ramblings by an old man. I think we should leave Monsieur Thermaine for the present, and concentrate all our efforts on finding this Maria Constantine. We know that Jacob was afraid of returning to this area, and we also now know that Thermaine first came to Hereford when he arrived in this country in 1860, if the old man's memory is to be believed. He probably set up a studio of some sort in the city where he no doubt advertised his services as an artist, hoping to secure commissions from the gentry. Maria Constantine must have been one of his clients,' said Ravenscroft, staring at the miniature in the locket.

'That would make the portrait just over thirty years old.'

'Yes, Tom. Maria must have been around twenty when the commission was undertaken. She would be around fifty years of age by now, if she's still alive.'

'Constantine could have been her maiden name.'

'If that's the case, then we'll have no chance of finding her.'

'Unless the lady never married.'

'You could be right, Tom. Pass me the Herefordshire *Post Office Directory*. There's just a remote possibility that we might find her still listed within its pages.'

Crabb searched through the row of books on the shelf in the corner of the room of the police station. 'It's two years out of date.'

'Never mind; it may still give us the information we require,' said Ravenscroft, turning over the pages of the red volume. 'Ah, here we are. 'Mr Francis Constantine. Miss

Maria Constantine. The Verzons, Ashperton.'
Good lord, that's only about five or six miles
or so from here.'

'I've seen that Verzons. It's that large house
on the side of the road, just before you reach
the crossroads at Trumpet,' said Crabb.

'I know the one you mean. We must have
passed by it several times on our way to
Hereford. Quickly, Tom, saddle the horse. We
shall proceed with all haste. Let's hope that
this is the vital information we seek. With
luck, we'll discover that Maria Constantine is
still alive, and that she can identify the locket
as once having belonged to her.'

★ ★ ★

Crabb turned the trap off the main road and
into the courtyard of the large Georgian
house.

'A fine building,' remarked Ravenscroft as
he stepped out of the horse-drawn vehicle.

'I think someone has noticed our arrival,
sir,' said Crabb.

Ravenscroft turned to see a stout, ruddy-
faced middle-aged man wearing a tweed suit
and waistcoat walking towards them, a large
sheep dog at his side. 'Good day to you, sir. I
believe this to be The Verzons?'

'You are correct, sir,' answered the man.

'I'm looking for Mr Francis Constantine.'

'Well you've found him.'

'I understand that a Miss Maria Constantine also resides here?'

'She does. She's my sister,' replied the man, giving Ravenscroft a suspicious look.

'Excellent. My name is Ravenscroft. I'm a detective police inspector in Ledbury.'

'I knows who you are.'

'I see. This is my colleague, Constable Crabb. I would be obliged if you and your sister could give us a few moments of your time.'

'What for?' asked the landowner bluntly.

'I would prefer to speak with both you and your sister, if I may.'

'I can't think why.'

'It is a matter of great importance, I can assure you,' persisted Ravenscroft.

'You'd best come in, then.'

'Thank you, Mr Constantine.'

'Stay, Brutus!' commanded the man, addressing the sheepdog, which lay down in the yard as its owner led the way through the main entrance of the building.

'Where's your mistress?' Constantine enquired of a young maid who came running towards the door.

'In the parlour, sir,' replied the maid.

'Follow me, gentlemen,' instructed Constantine.

Ravenscroft and Crabb followed the landowner through an inner door and found themselves being taken into a small room on the right of the building. As he entered, Ravenscroft noticed that a woman sat at the table, her back towards him, who appeared to be engaged in undertaking some kind of needlework.

'Police to see us,' said Constantine.

The woman stood up, and as she turned, Ravenscroft realised that he had found the woman he was seeking. Although her face was now lined and aged, it had nevertheless retained the same beauty, elegance and mystery that he had found within the portrait.

'Says his name is Ravenscroft, and that he must speak with both of us,' continued Constantine. 'He's the police from Ledbury.'

'Mr Ravenscroft,' answered the woman, somewhat startled by the unexpected arrivals.

'Forgive the intrusion, Miss Constantine,' replied Ravenscroft somewhat hesitantly, as he realised that he was staring at his hostess. 'Detective Inspector Ravenscroft, and this is my associate, Constable Crabb.'

'You'd better take a seat, gentlemen. Perhaps you'd care for some tea?'

'No thank you, that won't be necessary,' replied Ravenscroft, looking round the room. It seemed to him to emit both a comfort and keen attention to detail that its owner must have carefully bestowed upon it over the years, so that to him it almost resembled a kind of sanctuary, a retreat from the outside world.

'Now then, Ravenscroft, I hope you haven't come about my sheepdogs. That confounded fellow down the road, Martin, is always complaining; nothing better to do with his time.'

'No, Mr Constantine, it is not about your dogs,' said Ravenscroft, reaching into his pocket as he accepted the seat that had been offered.

'Always complaining about the dogs, he is. The man's an interfering busybody. Don't know why he can't just leave people alone,' muttered the farmer.

'I would be obliged, Miss Constantine, if you'd take a look at this for me,' said Ravenscroft, ignoring the man's remarks as he passed over the locket.

'Oh my God!' exclaimed Maria Constantine, turning a deathly white as she opened the locket.

'What is it, my dear?' asked her brother as he came forward and peered over her shoulder at the open locket. 'What is it that ails you, Maria?'

'I would be grateful if you'd confirm that

you are the same Maria depicted in the locket,' said Ravenscroft, observing its owner closely.

'Good grief!' exclaimed Constantine. 'I remember you having that done in Hereford all those years ago, by that funny French fellow.'

'Monsieur Louis Thermaine,' said Ravenscroft. 'So you can confirm its identity?'

'Yes, yes,' answered Maria Constantine in scarcely a whisper. Ravenscroft observed that her hands were shaking as she stared down at the portrait.

'Said you lost it in the hayfields, if I recall,' offered Constantine, walking over to the fireplace. 'Fancy it turning up after all this time.'

'Can you confirm that, Miss Constantine? When was the locket lost?' asked Ravenscroft.

'Yes. It was lost shortly after I had it commissioned. I think it was in 1861,' she answered. 'Where did you find it?'

Ravenscroft hesitated for a moment, seeing the look of fear and distress in her face, and not wanting to break the news of how he had come into possession of the locket.

'Well come on, man, where did you find it?' asked an impatient Francis Constantine.

'What I have to tell you, Miss Constantine, may be very distressing for you to hear. Three weeks ago the body of a man was found hanging from a tree on Hangman Hill in the Malvern Hills,' began Ravenscroft, trying to speak as calmly as he could.

'Good lord. The poor fellow,' exclaimed Constantine.

'Unfortunately, the man had been killed in a brutal fashion. At first we were unable to identify him, but by a chance encounter we discovered that he had been travelling with a visiting fair, at present in Ledbury. He went by the name of Jacob. When we made a search of the dead man's possessions, we found this locket.'

'Oh my God!' exclaimed Maria, bringing her hands towards her ashen face as her eyes began to fill with tears.

'There, Maria, don't distress yourself so,' said a startled Constantine, placing his hand on his sister's shoulders. 'It's distressing and all that, but don't fret so. It is not as though you knew the fellow.'

'I apologise for any distress caused, Miss Constantine, but can you tell me whether you might have known this man, Jacob? We estimate that he must have been nearly thirty years in age. Apparently he had been working in New York when he joined the fair-folk there.'

'No, no,' answered Maria, trying to control

her tears as she turned away.

'We've never been to New York, so how would we have known this man?' protested the farmer.

'We believe he may have originated from Herefordshire,' said Ravenscroft.

'Jacob, you say? He means nothing to me.'

'Miss Constantine?' asked Ravenscroft, leaning forward towards the unhappy woman.

'No, no,' she replied in scarcely a whisper.

'Fellow must have picked up the locket shortly after you lost it, Maria,' suggested Constantine.

'That is possible,' said Ravenscroft. 'I'm sorry to ask you again, but can you confirm that you lost the locket all those years ago? You didn't give it to anyone, as a kind of keepsake or as an act of remembrance?' he asked, anxious to know more about the locket and its owner.

'No; it is as my brother has just said. I was foolish enough to lose the locket in one of the fields. It was very clumsy of me,' answered Maria, dabbing her eyes with her handkerchief as she attempted to control her emotions.

'Thank you, Miss Constantine. I'm sorry to have caused you any distress. I must ask you for the return of the locket, if you will,' said Ravenscroft.

'Surely I may keep it, after all these years,'

pleaded Maria, looking up into Ravenscroft's eyes.

'I'm afraid I must retain it for the present, as it's police evidence, and may be required for further identification. However, I'm sure that once this case has been bought to a satisfactory conclusion, the locket will be returned to you as its rightful owner.'

The inspector saw the look of deep sadness in Maria's eyes as she reluctantly returned the locket. 'Thank you, Miss Constantine,' he said, standing up. 'Just one more question. How long after the portrait was commissioned did you realise that you'd lost it?'

'A few months, maybe a year; I can't remember.'

'Did you ever loan the locket to anyone?'

'No. Why should I?'

'Look, Ravenscroft, all this has been most upsetting for my sister. We've answered your questions. The prodigal locket has returned to the fold. Can't see why you can't return it to my sister now,' said Constantine.

'Thank you, Miss Constantine. We'll take our leave of you,' said Ravenscroft, ignoring the farmer's last remarks. 'If either of you can think of anything that will assist us in our investigations, we can be contacted at the police station in Ledbury.'

'I'll show you out,' said Constantine.

* * *

'She's lying to us,' said Ravenscroft as the trap made its way back to Ludlow.

'She certainly went a deathly colour when you produced that locket,' remarked Crabb. 'I thought the poor woman was going to faint.'

'Yes, you would have thought that she'd be overjoyed to know that her locket had been found once more. I don't believe that story about losing it in the hayfields all those years ago. I think she gave it to someone, someone who was very dear to her at that time.'

'You mean Jacob? He would only have been an infant then.'

'No, I don't think it would have been Jacob. It was probably given to someone else, a lover perhaps.'

'She must have thought, when she saw the locket, that whoever she gave it to must have died.'

'I believe you're correct, Tom. When she parted with the locket, she must have expected that she would see neither it, nor its new owner, ever again. I wonder who she gave it to. Why did she want to make us believe that she'd lost it in the hayfields all those years ago, a story which her brother also substantiated?'

'She was covering up for something that happened then.'

'Of course — she must have made up the story at the time, and told her brother of her loss. But why? Why did she not tell the truth and admit that she'd given it to a lover or friend?'

'Because she knew that her brother would not approve of her conduct in regard to the matter?'

'Indeed. That would explain why she still had to keep up that pretence, even now after all these years. She's still protecting this other person. Damn it! Our lives would be much easier if people just told us the truth. If only she'd told us who she'd given the locket to all those years ago, we might now be making some progress with finding Jacob's murderers. Of course, there's another possibility we have not yet considered.'

'What is that, sir?'

'That whoever Maria Constantine gave that locket to has either died or mislaid it in the intervening years. Jacob could then have found the locket, or inherited it from someone, or even stolen it, in which case we're following this case from the wrong direction. Jacob may have had no connection at all with Maria Constantine or Louis Thermaine. It could have been a mere coincidence that the locket was found amongst his effects.'

'But you don't really believe that, do you, sir?'

'No, I don't. I still think that there's a connection somewhere between Jacob and Maria Constantine.'

'Do you think that Francis Constantine could have killed Jacob?'

'To protect his sister, you mean? I can't see that, but at this stage of our investigations we can't discount any possibility. If only we knew why Jacob was afraid of returning to this area — and what the devil he was doing in America in the first place. The fair-folk are still in Ledbury for another night; let's have one more attempt before they leave to see if we can obtain any further information about Jacob.'

★   ★   ★

The daylight had begun to fade as Ravenscroft and Crabb made their way through the noisy excited crowds who thronged the streets of Ledbury.

'The man who runs the fair is called Tom Walker,' said Crabb.

'Then let's start with him,' said Ravenscroft.

'That's him over there, on the wheel of fortune.'

'Mr Walker?' said Ravenscroft, walking over towards a heavily built, unshaven, casually

65

dressed showman who was in the process of dealing out some cards to a group of men. 'I wonder whether I might have a word with you. My name is Detective Inspector Ravenscroft.'

'Your constable there interviewed me earlier today. I've told him all that I knows. Now then, ladies and gentlemen, last cards before we spin the lucky wheel!'

'Nevertheless, I would be grateful for a few further minutes of your time. It's a serious matter we are investigating,' persisted Ravenscroft.

'Here we go! Who will be the lucky winner this time?' said Walker, ignoring Ravenscroft as he spun the wheel. 'Ah, sorry, ladies and gentlemen, this would appear not to be your lucky chance.'

'Mr Walker, I must insist,' shouted Ravenscroft above the noise of a group of revellers who nearly collided with him.

'All right, all right,' grumbled Walker. 'Sorry, folks, stall is closed for the next few minutes. Blame it on the law.'

'Thank you,' said Ravenscroft as the men let out cries of disappointment before they drifted reluctantly away.

'Now, what do you want to know?' said the showman, drawing himself up to his full height and glaring directly into Ravenscroft's face.

'We understand that the fair was in America last year?'

'No, we've never been to America. Whatever gave you that idea?'

'Doctor Rockstone told us that he and the man Jacob were in America with the fair, before it came to this country.'

'Well Rockstone got it wrong, didn't he?' growled Walker.

'So you were not in America last year?'

'This fair has always been in England.'

'So when did Rockstone and Jacob join?'

'About six months ago.'

'Where did they join?'

'In Birmingham, I think. Look, is this going to take all night? I've got a livelihood to keep up.'

'We won't detain you more than is necessary, Mr Walker. So Rockstone and Jacob joined the fair together?'

'That's what I said.'

'Did Rockstone ever mention New York, or how he met Jacob?' continued Ravenscroft, determined to know more.

'They just said they'd recently travelled over from New York. Came over on one of them old Cunard ships, they said. They just wanted to join the fair.'

'So you let them?'

'Why should I not? They pays me a fee to

be with us, so why should I turn them away?'

'We believe Jacob came from this area.'

'I wouldn't know where he came from.'

'He never mentioned it to you?'

'No. Look, what is all this?' asked Walker, becoming more and more red in the face as his responses grew louder and more aggressive in tone.

'Surely Jacob must have said something about his past?'

'He said nothing. Kept very much to himself, he did. He never said more than a dozen words to me the whole time he were here.'

'We believe that Jacob didn't want the fair to go to Hereford. Why was that?'

'First I've heard of this,' snapped the showman.

'According to Mr Rockstone, Jacob was frightened that something would happen to him if the fair went there.'

'As I've just said, I knew nothing about this.'

'Then we'll have to ask Mr Rockstone. Where is the gentleman?'

'You won't find him here. He left early this morning.'

'Left this morning!' exclaimed Ravenscroft.

'That's what I said. Have you done? Now let me get on,' said Walker, turning away.

'That was rather sudden, wasn't it?'

'Folk come and go all the time; it's the nature of the fair business. Roll up, ladies and gentlemen! Come and try your luck on the wheel of fortune. There's one whole gold sovereign to be given away tonight to one lucky winner!'

'Did he say where he was going?' shouted out Ravenscroft over the noise of the boisterous new arrivals.

'Why would he tell me? Thank you, sir, just tuppence a go!'

'Did he leave anything behind?'

'He took everything with him. I thank you, madam. Thank you, sir.'

'What about the young boy who acted as his stooge in the audience?' asked Crabb.

'He went with him as well. Come on folks, come and try your luck on the wheel of fortune!'

'Thank you, Mr Walker. Come on, Tom; we can do nothing further here tonight,' said an annoyed Ravenscroft, walking away.

'What do we do now, sir?' asked Crabb.

'Issue a description of this Rockstone and send it to all the local police stations. Confound it, Tom. We should have taken him into custody last night!'

4

Ledbury

'What will you do now?' asked Lucy the following morning as she and her husband sat together at the breakfast table.

'Try and track down that quack doctor, Rockstone. He can't have got far.'

'Do you think he might have killed Jacob? He certainly seemed an unpleasant man.'

'I don't really know, but the fact that he left the town in a hurry tends to suggest that he knows a lot more about the dead man than he's told us. He may have been responsible for his murder; but if so, I can't see the motive, or why he would have gone to all that trouble of hanging Jacob on Hangman Hill. There may be another reason for his hasty departure — perhaps he may be a wanted man, and was afraid that if we questioned him further, his past crimes would have come to light. Either way, I don't think this case can proceed until we've apprehended him,' said Ravenscroft before taking another bite from his piece of toast.

'He could have left town by train,' suggested Lucy.

'That is a possibility. After I've finished breakfast, I'll take a walk up to the station. If they remember him leaving, they might be able to tell me the destination of his ticket. Failing that, Tom and I will go round the local inns to see if he took one of the horses. Then there are the local cab men to interview; one of them may have taken Rockstone out of the town.'

'It seems that you'll have quite a busy day. This Maria Constantine seems quite intriguing.'

'I only wish she'd felt inclined to have been more forthcoming concerning that locket. I'm sure she gave it to someone all those years ago, and doesn't want either her brother or ourselves to know who it was.'

'You'll have to take her in for more questioning,' suggested Lucy, pouring out another cup of tea.

'I'm not sure that would do any good at this stage. I don't think she'd tell us anything concerning the man Jacob and how he might have acquired the locket. She was certainly distressed when I produced it. It obviously meant a great deal to her. I could almost feel her pain and suffering,' said Ravenscroft thoughtfully.

'I think you're quite taken by this Maria

Constantine,' teased Lucy.

'I can assure you, my dear, that you have nothing to fear on that score. I am utterly devoted to you. But yes, she is certainly an intriguing person, and I'd be interested to know more about her. Anyway, we need to track down that charlatan Rockstone, so I'll bid you good day, my dear,' said Ravenscroft, pushing aside his plate as he rose from the breakfast table.

'I wish you success with your search,' said Lucy with a smile as her husband left the room.

★   ★   ★

Later that morning, Lucy was busily engaged in arranging some flowers on the hall table when there came a knock on the front door.

'Don't worry, Susan; I'll see to it,' she called out. 'I expect it's only the butcher's boy come to see about the order.'

She opened the door to discover a middle-aged woman wearing a long overcoat and shawl standing before her.

'Oh, I am sorry to disturb you. I was looking for Inspector Ravenscroft. I've just called at the police station and they thought he might be here,' said the woman somewhat apprehensively.

'I'm afraid my husband is away on business at present,' replied Lucy, straining to see the woman's face, which was partly covered by her bonnet that was pulled low. 'Perhaps you would care to call later?'

'I'm afraid I can't do that. I'll call another day,' said the woman, quickly turning away.

'Who shall I say has called?'

'It's no matter. I'm sorry for the intrusion,' said the stranger, beginning to walk away from the cottage.

'Please don't go. You are Miss Constantine, if I'm not mistaken. I am Mrs Ravenscroft. Please do come inside,' called out Lucy.

'Yes, I am Maria Constantine,' replied the woman hesitantly. 'How did you know my name?'

'My husband showed me the locket and mentioned that he had called upon you yesterday,' said Lucy, smiling.

'Oh yes, the locket.'

'Do please come inside,' repeated Lucy, hoping that the new arrival would accept her offer.

The woman looked down nervously at her shoes.

'Please.'

'Thank you.'

'Do come this way,' said Lucy, indicating that her guest should step inside.

73

'You are most kind.'

'May I take your bonnet?'

'Thank you.'

'Do please take a seat. Can I offer you some refreshment?'

'No, thank you. I'm sorry for the intrusion,' said the visitor, seating herself on one of the chairs.

'It is no intrusion, I can assure you.'

'So your husband told you of his visit to The Verzons yesterday?'

'Yes, he said that he met you and your brother.' Lucy smiled again, hoping that she could put her unsettled guest at her ease.

'I am afraid that I was not very forthcoming in answering your husband's questions. He must have thought me quite rude.'

'I believe that my husband is used to asking a great many questions in his line of work.'

'There were things that I couldn't say in front of my brother,' said Maria, looking away.

'I understand,' replied Lucy, having noticed the sadness in the other's eyes.

'Do you? I wonder. Oh, I am sorry — I shouldn't have said that. I don't wish to cause any offence when you've been so kind as to invite me into your home. Perhaps I should go,' said Maria, suddenly rising from her chair.

'I can assure you, Miss Constantine, that

you haven't caused any offence,' said Lucy, placing her hand on the woman's arm. 'I appreciate that it can sometimes be very difficult to talk. I trust that you will stay. I can assure you that whatever you have to tell me will be held in the highest confidence.'

'You're very kind,' replied Maria, regaining her seat and staring into Lucy's eyes. 'I believe that you're a woman of this world, and that I may trust you.'

'You have my word. Perhaps you'd like a glass of water?'

'No, thank you. I can't stay long. My brother is conducting some business in the town, and we are to meet up shortly in the marketplace.'

'Of course. I understand.'

'My story, Mrs Ravenscroft, is not a happy one, and I am now afraid of what the consequences may be should I be forthcoming in the telling of it. Nevertheless, I know that I will not be able to rest until my greatest fears have been confirmed. I am sorry if I'm not speaking coherently.'

'Please take your time,' said Lucy reassuringly.

'Many years ago I committed a foolish indiscretion.' Maria then paused and stared out of the window. Lucy looked down at her hands in her lap, knowing that all she now had to do was to remain silent, until her guest acquired the confidence to continue.

'It was in 1862. I found myself with child. I couldn't tell either my parents or my brother. It would have destroyed them — the scandal, the ruination of our name, our standing in society.'

'I understand,' sympathised Lucy, remembering her own previous unhappy circumstances.

'For some months I kept my secret from all, but then I realised that I would have to leave The Verzons before others guessed my secret. I made up some pretext about wanting to travel abroad for several months with an old school friend of mine. Instead I came to London and rented some rooms in a rather unpleasant boarding house that provided accommodation for distressed fallen women such as myself. My son was born. He was the most beautiful baby I had ever seen. I named him Christopher.' Tears began to form in Maria's eyes.

'Christopher. That's such a nice name,' said Lucy.

'Do you think so?'

'Yes I do.'

'I thought so as well. He was my son, and I was his mother, and I loved him so; but I knew that I could never take him back to The Verzons. What I did next, I have regretted for every day of my life ever since.'

76

Lucy, fearing the outcome of her guest's story, leaned forward and again placed her hand on the other's wrist.

'I did something quite terrible, Mrs Ravenscroft. I went to Coram's Fields and gave away my child to the Foundling Hospital. Please don't judge me too harshly.'

'No, I could never do that,' stuttered Lucy, not knowing whether she had said the right thing or not.

'I gave away my darling Christopher to the Foundling Hospital!' repeated Maria, the tears beginning to fall from her eyes.

'Here, please take this,' said Lucy, handing a handkerchief to the distressed woman.

'Thank you. You're so very kind. You're the only person I have ever spoken to about this in all these years. It has been so difficult. It was all I could do at the time; you must see that. I believed the hospital would give my son the start in life that he deserved, and which I could never provide for him. I said to myself that one day, when my parents had died and my brother was married, I would return to the hospital and claim back my dear child. That's when I parted with the locket. I gave it to the hospital as a kind of token. Apparently that was what the mothers did: they left tokens with the children, so that one day they could return and reclaim that which

77

they had given away. I hoped that as my child grew older he would open that locket, and look down at that portrait, and know that it was his mother there who loved him so much and who would never forget him.' Maria paused from her narrative and dabbed her eyes on the handkerchief. 'You don't think that I was cruel?' she suddenly cried out. 'You'll judge me for my heartlessness.'

'No. You did what was best at the time.'

'Yes, I've told myself that a great deal over the years, but it's done nothing to assuage my guilt. How can I have been so thoughtless?'

'So you were never able to return to the Foundling Hospital?' asked Lucy after a few moments of silence had elapsed.

'No. My parents died seven and five years ago respectively. My brother had never married during the intervening years, but by then it was too late. I knew that my son would have grown up over the years, that he would have left the hospital, and that he would have become a man. At night I would lie awake wondering what had become of him. Perhaps he had become a lawyer, a soldier, a clergyman; that he had become prosperous; even married and had children of his own. I worried, however, that my actions may have blighted his life, and that his future had been cursed by my act of foolishness.

How was I to know? Then yesterday your husband visited us at The Verzons, and it seemed that my world had come to an end when he told me of the dead man, and how they had found the locket amongst his possessions!' said Maria, becoming distressed.

'We cannot be sure that the dead man, Jacob, was your son. The locket could have been given to him by your Christopher,' suggested Lucy, hoping to calm the other's fears.

'No, he would never have done that. He would never have given away the locket,' said Maria, as Lucy again saw the pain in her eyes.

'Your son may have lost the locket, and the man Jacob found it.'

'Do you think so, Mrs Ravenscroft?'

'Lucy.'

'Lucy.'

'The locket could have been stolen by Jacob. So Jacob may not have been your son. Your son could still be alive.'

'Yes, yes, he is still alive. Pray that he is still alive. Tell me that he is still alive!'

'We just don't know at present. My husband is making enquiries concerning a man called Rockstone, an American. Apparently Jacob was working in America when he met this Rockstone, and he then sought employment with him.'

'My son went to America?'

'Jacob went to America. But as I said, Miss Constantine, we don't know that Jacob and your son were the same man. All we know at present is that Rockstone and Jacob went to England, where they joined a travelling fair.'

'A fair? I don't quite understand.'

'Yes. Rockstone was, or rather is, a travelling showman who sells quack medicines to unsuspecting people, and Jacob was his assistant. Rockstone left the fair in a hurry yesterday, and my husband is desperately trying to find him.'

'I see,' said Maria, handing back the handkerchief to Lucy.

'I'm sure that once my husband has found this man, he'll be able to tell us more about Jacob.'

'Yes, yes. So you think that my son may be alive?'

'I don't know, Miss Constantine.'

'Maria.'

'Maria. At the present we have no way of knowing whether your son is alive or dead. But I can assure you that I, or rather my husband and I, will do all that is within our power to obtain the truth.'

'You're so very kind, Mrs Ravenscroft. Lucy.'

'As soon as we know anything, you can be certain that we'll inform you of the outcome.'

'Thank you, but you must not come to The Verzons. I can't let my brother know the truth. He would never forgive me,' said an anxious Maria, rising from her seat.

'Then I shall write.'

'Yes, yes, that would be better.'

'You would have no objection if I told my husband of our meeting?' asked Lucy. 'If we are to find your son, he must know everything that you've just told me.'

'No, I appreciate what you're saying. You've been so very kind, but I must leave now. My brother will be wondering what's become of me.'

'Maria, perhaps you should talk with your brother. You may find that he's more understanding and sympathetic to your predicament than you had previously thought.'

'No, I could never do that. You wouldn't say that if you knew my brother,' said Maria, shaking her head. 'He would become very angry. I know that. He'd cast me out.'

'I am sorry; I have been somewhat presumptuous. Maria, rest assured that we will do everything we can to find out the truth,' said Lucy, taking the other's hands.

'Thank you.'

'Have faith.'

'Confound it, Tom, where has the fellow gone?' said a frustrated Ravenscroft as he walked into the police station in Ledbury later that afternoon.

'Perhaps he met up with someone,' suggested Crabb, not quite knowing what to say to soften his superior's annoyance.

'Well, the ticket office at the station has no record of him leaving the town by train, the hostelries have no recollection of hiring out a horse to the man, and not one of the cab drivers can remember taking a fare with anyone fitting his description. The man cannot just have walked out of town; it's quite a distance to either Hereford or Malvern. So I believe you must be correct, Tom. But if Rockstone did meet up with someone, who was that person? I suppose there's another possibility.'

'What is that, sir?'

'Rockstone is hiding somewhere locally, in some barn or outhouse, or even in the woods.'

'He could still be with the fair.'

'You may be right. Walker could have been lying to us. Knowing that we were about to return, the fair-folk may have taken it upon themselves to hide Rockstone. I think we should make a thorough search of the carts and tents tonight before they leave,' said a weary Ravenscroft, sinking into his chair and raising his feet onto the desk. 'Take a seat, Tom. The fair can wait for a few minutes.'

'Thank you, sir,' said Crabb, grateful to be complying with the request.

'What the deuce!' Ravenscroft suddenly exclaimed. 'The drawer of this desk has been forced open!'

Crabb hurried round to inspect the damage.

'See here, Tom — there are the marks where someone has inserted a sharp implement to force open the lock on the drawer.'

'There was nothing of value in there,' said Crabb.

'Only those photographs we took of the dead man in the morgue. They've been stolen! Why the blazes would anyone want to break into the station here and remove those photographs?'

'Shall I have a look round and see if anything else has been taken?'

'You can, but I think we'll find that it's only the photographs that have been removed. What on earth would anyone want with the photographs of a dead man? Of course — to stop us having any record of Jacob and what he looked like.'

'Well we can't take any more photographs,' said Crabb. 'We buried him two weeks ago in that plot in Little Malvern churchyard.'

'Exactly. But by stealing our only photographic record of Jacob, it seems as if the thief was anxious that no one else should ever see them. Without a photograph, no one in the future will be able to identify the dead man. But who stole them?'

'Rockstone? Whilst we were out looking for him, he may have crept in here and removed the photographs.'

'Yes, that seems the most likely thing, unless there's somebody else, at present unknown to us, who has taken them. It's as if someone doesn't want us to find out about Jacob, for fear of what we might discover.'

'There might still be the original photographic plates,' suggested Crabb. 'We could make further copies.'

'Of course. Who took the photographs?'

'Lancing in the Homend, I believe.'

'Right, then we'll see if Mr Lancing still has the plates. Let's hope that he hasn't destroyed them. We may yet be able to acquire further copies, as you say. After which we'll make a thorough search of the fair. If they're hiding Rockstone, I mean to apprehend the man.'

★ ★ ★

A few minutes later, Ravenscroft and Crabb entered the premises of H. Lancing Photographers at the far end of the Homend.

'Thank goodness you've come!' cried out the distressed photographer, rushing forward to meet them.

'Whatever is the matter, Mr Lancing?' asked a concerned Ravenscroft.

'Do please come this way, gentlemen. Something quite terrible has happened,' replied the photographer, leading the way into an inner room.

'Good heavens!' exclaimed Crabb.

'All my photographic plates have been destroyed!' cried out Lancing, pointing to the piles of broken glass and other debris on the floor.

'When did this happen?' enquired Ravenscroft.

'Not ten minutes ago. I returned from an assignment in another part of town and entered my premises to find this state of destruction. Who can have carried out such a terrible thing? All my plates, totally irreplaceable; images lost forever for posterity. Who can have done such a thing, Inspector?'

'I am afraid I don't know, Mr Lancing,' said Ravenscroft.

'I sent the boy to fetch you as soon as I discovered what had happened.'

'We did not see the boy,' said Crabb.

'Then how did you know?'

'When we returned to the police station this afternoon, we discovered that the photographs you took of the dead man Jacob had been stolen from our premises,' explained Ravenscroft.

'Stolen?'

'Yes. Your name and details were on the backs of the photographs. Whoever took them was also intent on destroying the original plates.'

'But why do that?'

'I wish I could answer that question, Mr Lancing. It seems that someone has gone to a great deal of trouble to make sure that no photographic image of the dead man remains. Whoever committed this destruction clearly didn't have the time to go through all your plates to find the ones relating to Jacob. I'm very sorry for your loss.'

'Terrible! Why? Why?' continued the distraught photographer, running his hand through his white hair.

'I'll have a word with my superiors and see if we can recompense you in some way. After all, you did produce the photographs upon our instruction. As you said, this must have taken place within the last hour. When you returned, did you see anyone outside the premises, or in the vicinity, who might have been acting in a strange way?'

'No, I believe not — although I do now recall that I did pass by a man on the way down from the railway station. He seemed to be in quite a hurry.'

'Can you describe this man to us?'

'Well, he was quite tall, of thin stature, clean-shaven, dark-haired. That's all I can remember.'

'What age do you think he was?'

'Around forty or so, I suppose. He was dressed in a dark overcoat. His hat was pulled down over the top of his face, so I couldn't see his features clearly.'

'Do you think you may have seen this man before?'

'No. I'd say he wasn't a local man. But as I said, I couldn't see his face clearly.'

'Thank you, Mr Lancing. I'm sorry you've been caught up in all this trouble. We'll keep you informed of any developments in this case, and hopefully catch the person who committed this outrage.'

'This is all quite upsetting. I only wish I'd made further copies,' muttered the photographer and shaking his head as the two detectives made their way out of the shop.

* * *

'Poor Mr Lancing. And he's such a nice pleasant man as well,' said Lucy after she and her husband had each finished narrating their experiences of the day.

'It was just such wanton destruction. But why would the perpetrator of this deed want to prevent any photographic images of Jacob surviving?' said Ravenscroft, pouring himself another drink from the decanter.

'So he couldn't be identified?' suggested Lucy.

'Exactly. But who *was* Jacob, and why is someone now anxious to conceal his identity?'

'Perhaps that awful Rockstone is the culprit.'

'I thought so at first, but the description given by Mr Lancing of the man who was hurrying away from his premises doesn't seem to match Rockstone's appearance.'

'Rockstone could have an accomplice.'

'I suppose that's a possibility, particularly if this accomplice has been providing shelter for Rockstone. Tom and I made a thorough search of the carts and tents of the fairground folk, much to Mr Walker's displeasure I can tell you — at one stage I thought the man was going to assault us — but there was no Rockstone to be found. Until we've discovered the whereabouts of the American, I fear that we'll be unable to proceed further with this case.'

'Samuel, I do believe I might be able to help you,' suggested Lucy tentatively.

'Oh? How is that, my dear?'

'It relates to what Maria Constantine told me this morning.'

'Yes, that was certainly a heart-rending story.'

'From what she told me about giving away her son all those years ago, and leaving the locket with the Foundling Hospital as a kind of token for him, it would seem that if I were to visit the hospital tomorrow, I might be able to learn more about what became of him.'

'I don't think I could let you do that,' protested Ravenscroft.

'Whyever should I not? I'm quite capable of travelling up to London on my own. If the hospital could provide me with more information about Christopher, we might then know whether he was the dead man Jacob or not,' replied Lucy indignantly.

'That would be quite irregular. Anyway, I don't like the idea of you travelling alone.'

'Oh don't be so stuffy, Samuel. Nothing is going to happen to me. I would go straight up to London, secure a cab to the Foundling Hospital, find out the information we need, and then return home by the afternoon train.

I would be back before you knew that I'd gone,' pleaded Lucy.

'The authorities there might not be forthcoming with the information.'

'Why? Is it because I'm a woman?'

'No, that's not the reason. It's because you're not a member of the police force, and they would be reluctant to part with the information about this child Christopher.'

'But you could send them a telegram explaining why you are unable to come in person, requesting them to answer my questions. Oh please say yes, Samuel. If you'd seen how distressed that poor woman was, you would want to do everything in your power to assist her.'

'It was such a long time ago, my dear; and I fear that if Jacob really was her son Christopher, then it could prove even more upsetting for her. Sometimes the truth can be very painful to accept, and in certain situations it's kinder never to know what has really happened.'

'I can't believe you just said that!' exclaimed Lucy. 'As a detective, you have always sought out the truth, and I know you have never rested until you have drawn your various investigations to satisfactory conclusions. We — I — owe it to Maria Constantine to find out what happened to her son. I'm afraid if you won't give me your permission to go to London tomorrow, then I shall just have to go on my own.'

'I can see that you're quite determined to help Miss Constantine.'

'I am.'

'Then I think you should go.'

'Oh Samuel, thank you so much.'

'But only on one condition.'

'Yes, yes, anything,' replied Lucy eagerly.

'The condition is that you take the greatest of care; and no matter what you discover at the Foundling Hospital, you are to return home straight away so that we may discuss it together before deciding how to proceed further.' Ravenscroft smiled and took his wife's hands in his.

'Of course, Samuel. I would not do otherwise.'

5

London

'A fine day, I think. Don't you agree?'

Lucy looked up from her book.

'I'm so sorry. I didn't mean to disturb you. Please excuse me, ma'am.'

Lucy gave a brief smile at the tall middle-aged gentleman who sat opposite her in the carriage and then resumed her reading.

When she had joined the London-bound train at Ledbury station an hour previously, the compartment had been nearly full, her travelling companions consisting of a middle-aged red-faced country woman, a young child accompanied by his governess, a soldier, an elderly gentleman who had been content to retreat behind his copy of the day's *Times* newspaper, and the gentleman who had remarked on the condition of the weather. The country woman had departed at Worcester station, the soldier at Pershore, the elderly gentleman at Evesham, and the governess and her charge had now left the train at Moreton-in-the-Marsh.

'I always find this journey interesting. So

beautiful, the run over the Cotswolds,' said the man after a few minutes' silence had elapsed. 'Do you travel this way very often?'

'Very rarely,' replied Lucy, observing that the man had a strange but familiar accent.

'Once the train has left Reading, the journey presents little of value,' the man continued. 'I suppose you're travelling all the way to London?'

'Yes,' said Lucy, feeling uneasy in the other's presence and hoping that he would cease his questions as she resumed her reading.

'I'm travelling to the great metropolis as well. Although I hail originally from New Hampshire, I've lived over here in your delightful country for the past five years. Much as I like your countryside, and the quaint country towns of Herefordshire, I find it's always a relief to return to the pleasures of the capital. No offence to Ledbury, of course, which is a delightful place, but I should have no wish to become an inhabitant of the town.'

'I find it pleasant enough,' said Lucy formally, trusting that her offhand manner might deter the man from continuing further with the conversation.

'You've evidently lived there a long time.'

'About six or seven years,' replied Lucy, realising that perhaps she had said too much.

'I always believe that one can get the feel of

a place, and know whether one will be content there, within three hours of one's arrival,' said the man again. 'I knew that when I arrived in London. I knew that was the place for me.'

Lucy said nothing as she looked out of the window of the carriage. As the green fields and small villages passed by, she began to wonder whether this stranger, who spoke in the same manner as Rockstone and who had joined the train at Ledbury, might even have been an associate of the missing man. Feeling uncomfortable in his presence, she hoped the train would stop shortly and that they might be joined by other passengers.

The man coughed before producing a small black book from his coat pocket, which he appeared to be reading intently, much to Lucy's relief.

A few minutes later the train pulled into the busy station at Oxford, and Lucy was relieved to see a young couple entering their compartment.

Just over an hour later the train drew into Paddington station, and Lucy alighted from the carriage. As she walked along the busy platform, thronged with numerous people all seemingly anxious to begin their business for the day in the great metropolis, she became aware that the American was walking closely behind her. Reaching the cab rank at the back of the station, she joined the line of arrivals.

'Rather a long line, I fear,' said the American with a smile as he stood at her side. 'Perhaps we'll do much better if we share a cab. May I ask where you're going, my good lady?'

'That, sir, is no business of yours. And no, I have no desire to share a cab,' replied Lucy firmly.

'I'm sorry, ma'am. I didn't wish to cause any offence.'

Lucy said nothing as she anxiously sought to attract the attention of one of the cabmen. As the queue gradually edged forward, she turned, and was pleased to see that the stranger was nowhere to be seen.

'Where would you like to go to, madam?' enquired a cheery cabman.

'Russel Square if you please, and then on to the Foundling Hospital.'

'Right you are. Have you there in just fifteen minutes.'

* * *

Lucy alighted from the cab, and after paying the man his due, looked across to the fine, elegant Georgian house with its two extensions protruding outwards on either side.

Although she observed that a number of trees stood in the near vicinity, and that a group of young girls, each wearing a uniform with a white pinafore and cap, were engaged in playing a game of leapfrog on the grass, such an idyllic scene was somewhat spoiled by the appearance of a cloud of thick black smoke that drifted over the whole area.

Lucy walked the few steps to the front door but turned before reaching out for the bell pull, almost expecting to see again the stranger from the train, but was relieved to find that no one of his description was in the locality.

'Can I be of assistance to you, ma'am?' asked a young girl, giving a curtsey before her.

'I have an appointment to see the guardian of the Foundling Hospital,' said Lucy, smiling.

'That will be Doctor March. If you'd care to come and follow me this way, ma'am?' The girl curtseyed once more.

Lucy entered the building and followed the girl up a long winding staircase, the walls of which were adorned with fine eighteenth-century portraits.

'Who shall I say it is, ma'am?' asked the girl, tapping on a door to the left of the top of the stairs.

'Mrs Ravenscroft.'

'Enter!' called out a voice from within.

'Mrs Ravenscroft to see you, sir,' announced the girl.

'Ah, Mrs Ravenscroft. Do please come in,' said an elderly grey-haired gentleman rising from his desk and crossing over to the door. 'Thank you, Mary. You may go.'

'Yes, sir.' She curtseyed once more before leaving the room and closing the door behind her.

'Mary is such a pleasant girl. One of our foundlings, of course, but also one of our greatest successes. She will shortly be leaving us, but I believe she will do well in her new situation,' said March. 'Do please take a seat, Mrs Ravenscroft.'

'Thank you,' replied Lucy, looking around the fine room with its ornate cornices, bookcases and portraits, before accepting the chair.

'Now then, Mrs Ravenscroft. I am in receipt of your husband's telegram, received earlier this morning,' said March, sitting down at the other side of the desk and peering at the form through a pair of heavy spectacles. 'But I have to tell you that this is most irregular, most irregular indeed.'

'Oh? Why is that, sir?' asked Lucy, feeling somewhat overawed by both the impressive room and its occupant.

'Your husband says here that he is unable to come in person, as he is detained on urgent police business, and that he has sent you in his place, as you are involved in the case,' continued March in a dryly formal tone of voice.

'That is so.'

'You gave up a child to the Foundling Hospital?' asked March, peering over the top of his spectacles.

'Oh no, sir. I'm acting on behalf of another lady.'

'I see. Well, I don't think that the foundation can be of any help to you. When our mothers leave their children in our care, they do so with the assurance that both the identity of the child and its mother will remain strictly confidential. I'm sorry that you have had a wasted journey,' said the doctor, closing the telegram and tossing it onto the desk.

'No, sir; I'm afraid you don't quite understand the reason for my visit,' protested Lucy.

'Then perhaps you should enlighten me, Mrs Ravenscroft.'

'The matter is of serious concern. A few weeks ago a man was found dead on one of the hills, near where my husband and I live.

He had been killed in a most brutal manner. My husband was unable to identify this man, but was able to recover this item from his effects,' said Lucy, taking out the locket from her handbag and placing it on the desk in front of March.

'I see,' replied the doctor, picking up the locket and examining it with a degree of caution.

'If you open the locket, you will observe a portrait of a lady inside,' instructed Lucy.

'Quite a striking portrait, but I still don't see what this has to do with the Foundling Hospital.'

'My husband, Inspector Ravenscroft, was able to identify the artist, and upon visiting him was also able to ascertain the name of the lady depicted there.'

'Go on,' said March, beginning to show an interest.

'We were then able to find the lady in question. Yesterday she visited me and told me a very sad story. Many years ago she committed a serious indiscretion, and a child was born. Finding herself unable to take her child home, she entrusted it to the care of your hospital.'

'I see.'

'The lady left the locket with the child.'

'Ah yes, that's what a great many of our

mothers have done in the past. They left a token with the hospital so that if their personal circumstances changed in the future, they could return to reclaim the child.'

'And do many of the mothers do that?'

'I'm afraid that only a small number are able to do so. When a child is admitted here, we give it a new identity and name, so that it may also be given a fresh start in life. Although this is all very interesting, I still don't see how I can assist you, Mrs Ravenscroft. Why hasn't the woman in question come forward to take back her child?'

'All of this happened a long time ago; nearly thirty years ago, in fact.'

'I see.'

'The lady in question could never have taken back her child because of the difficulty of her situation. But now that she has seen the locket, she is most anxious to know what happened to her child. My husband is also most concerned to establish the identity of the dead man. Without that information, he feels that he may never be able to bring his murderers to justice,' said Lucy, leaning forward as she sought to press home her case.

'Yes, I can see all of this, but it is still most irregular. It's all a question of confidentiality, you must understand.'

'I appreciate what you're saying. But the child must have left the hospital many years ago, and the lady in person has given me permission to act on her behalf. If you knew this lady, Doctor March, you would have witnessed the uncertainty and pain this case has caused her. She does not know whether her child is still alive, or whether he was the man who died on the hills. You're the only person who can be of help. You must have records of what happened to the children?' pleaded Lucy.

'Yes, we do have records.'

'Then I implore you, sir, to assist both the police and the lady in this case.'

March said nothing as he leaned back in his chair and looked up at the ceiling, deep in thought. Lucy recovered the locket from the top of the desk and placed it in her handbag, knowing that she could do no more.

'As this took place many years ago, as you said, it would do no harm, I suppose, to see what we can find out about this child — but only on the strict assurance that nothing of what you learn today will ever enter the public domain.'

Lucy nodded her head in agreement.

'When was the child admitted?' asked March, rising from his chair.

'In 1862 or early 1863, I believe.'

March walked over to one of the bookshelves and took down two large ledgers and placed them on the desk. 'These are the billet records that were compiled when a child was admitted. I think we'll start with this volume. Your search maybe very difficult, for we never record either the name of the mother or her baby in the records. The only way in which a mother could later reclaim her child would be to describe the token that she left behind originally. The column here gives descriptions of the tokens left, which were then attached to the child's billet, and this records the date of admission and the new name the child was given. Now let's see.'

For the next few minutes, Lucy looked down at the pages in the ledger as March turned over the sheets. She felt her heart beating loudly with the fear that their search might prove unfruitful.

'Ah, I think we may have found what you're looking for!' exclaimed March suddenly.

Lucy moved closer to the page in question.

'See there — November 21, 1862. Silver locket containing portrait entitled Maria.'

'That must be the one,' said an excited Lucy.

'Indeed so. The child was given the name Thomas Temple.'

'Not Jacob?' asked Lucy, feeling somewhat disappointed.

'No, Thomas Temple. Ah, I think I can see a connection. The children were often named after famous people. Our founder was Thomas Coram, and many of the boys were given the Christian name Thomas, in memory of the great man. In regard to surnames, a child could be named after a prominent person of the day. Henry John Temple was the British prime minister in 1862; you may remember him better by his title of 3rd Viscount Palmerston. The child certainly received a name to be proud of. But I can see, Mrs Ravenscroft, that you were hoping for another name to appear in the register. However, once a child obtained maturity, there would be nothing to stop them from changing their name to something more to their liking.'

'I understand. Is there any way we can tell what happened to the child?'

'Yes indeed. When a child reaches the age of fifteen, it is decided that they should leave the hospital. The girls are often found employment as maids, or in other areas of domestic service. Mary, the girl you saw earlier, will shortly be leaving us to take up a position in the household of one of our governors, where I believe she'll do quite well. The boys either join the army or navy as cadets, or are apprenticed to professional people such as bakers, merchants, tailors and so on. We endeavour to match the child's aptitude in each case. We have records of the governors' meetings when such decisions are made, together with copies of the apprentice indentures.'

'This is all most impressive, and to your credit,' remarked Lucy.

'Now let me see. If young Thomas was admitted in 1862, then he would have been ready to leave us in 1877. I myself was not appointed a governor here until two years later, so obviously I can't provide you with any recollection of the case,' said March, closing the billet book and replacing it on the shelf before running his fingers along another line of ledgers. 'Ah, here we are. 1877.'

Lucy watched as the doctor placed the ledger on the desk and began to thumb through the pages. 'Yes, here we are,' he announced after a few minutes had elapsed. 'Meeting of the governors, November 1877. Thomas Temple, having attained the age of fifteen, is to be apprenticed as a junior clerk to Mincing and Stricket, merchants and seedsmen of Limehouse, London.' It would seem that our young Thomas must have done well with his writing and arithmetic to be accorded such an opportunity in life.'

'So Thomas would have left the hospital then, in 1877?'

'Indeed.'

'Do we know what happened to him next?'

'Well, we know he must have gone to Mincing and Stricket. I can see no further mention of what might have happened to him after that, although I believe the hospital governors would have made a note in any of their further meetings had there been anything contrary to report,' said March, again turning over the pages.

'In what way?' enquired Lucy.

'If Mincing and Stricket had gone into insolvency, or if there was evidence that the apprentice had been ill used, if he had absconded, or if he had died, then there would have been a record made of the event. But looking through these pages, I can see no such evidence. I think we can conclude, therefore, that everything went well with young Thomas. And I'm afraid that is all I can tell you, Mrs Ravenscroft.'

'Thank you, Doctor March; you've been of great assistance to both my husband and myself. I wonder if you have any photographs of the young Thomas?'

'I'm afraid not.'

'Well, thank you again. I also know that

Thomas's mother will be pleased with what we've uncovered.'

'Indeed. May I ask what you'll do now, Mrs Ravenscroft?' asked March.

'I wonder if you have a copy of the *London Street Directory*?'

'Indeed,' said March, opening the drawer of his desk and taking out a large red volume. 'Now how can I help you?'

'Would you be so kind as to see whether Mincing and Stricket are still to be found in Limehouse?'

⋆ ⋆ ⋆

A few minutes later, Lucy alighted from the cab.

'You'd do well not to stay too long in this neighbourhood,' remarked the cabman as he accepted her payment.

'Whyever not?' enquired Lucy.

'There are some rather nasty individuals to be found loitering around the canal entrance down there. Want me to wait for you?'

'No, thank you. I don't quite know how long I'll be.'

'You should find what you're looking for down this road,' called out the cabman as he departed.

Lucy looked around her at the tall

buildings and warehouses that crowded in upon one another along the narrow street. Further in the distance she could see a row of old wooden houses of several storeys in construction that had clearly seen better days. To her left, between two of the warehouses, the river was lapping against the sides of the quay, as two or three dogs searched amongst piles of rubbish. A group of ragged children who had been playing near one of the buildings gave Lucy cold stares and disappeared rapidly down one of the nearby alleyways before she could engage them in conversation.

So this was where young Thomas Temple had come in 1877. He must have found this world so different from the close confines of the Foundling Hospital where he had been raised for the first fifteen years of his life. Lucy wondered whether he might still be working and living in the area, in which case her search would shortly be over; or whether he had moved on to a better world.

'Lady is lost?'

Lucy turned round to see a young Chinese girl looking up at her.

'Yes. I'm looking for Mincing and Stricket,' she replied, smiling at the girl, whom she estimated to be no more than seven or eight years of age.

'Down there.' The girl pointed to a narrow alleyway running off the street.

'Thank you,' said Lucy, handing a penny to the child.

The girl grasped the coin, gave a brief smile and then ran off.

Lucy made her way down the alleyway, looking at the entrances to the buildings on either side as she passed by, until she reached an old brick-built establishment that had a faded brass plate on its front door bearing the words 'Mincing and Stricket. Merchants.' Pushing open the door and cautiously entering the building, she found herself standing in a drab, darkened hallway. An old grey-haired man was engaged in writing in a ledger at a desk at the far end.

'Good morning. Do I have the honour of addressing either Mr Mincing or Mr Stricket?' asked Lucy, edging closer as her eyes slowly adjusted to the dim light.

The man said nothing as he resumed his writing, muttering to himself as he did so.

'Good morning. Mr Mincing?' repeated Lucy in a louder voice.

'Yes?' said the man, looking up from his labour and peering at her over the top of his glasses.

'My name is Mrs Ravenscroft.'

'What? I can't hear you,' said the man,

bringing his hand up to one of his ears.

'Mrs Ravenscroft,' said Lucy in an even louder voice.

'Can't hear you,' replied the man. 'Stricket, where are you?'

Lucy waited for a moment as an even older man shuffled into the room.

'Can't hear the lady,' muttered the first man, resuming his writing.

'Mr Mincing is rather hard of hearing,' said the new arrival. 'How I can help you? It isn't often we see such a lady as yourself in this area.'

'My name is Mrs Ravenscroft. I presume you are Mr Stricket?'

'I am indeed. What did you say your name was?'

'Ravenscroft.'

'Ravenscroft,' repeated the new arrival with great deliberation.

'I am making enquiries about one of your employees.'

'Oh yes?' said Stricket, suddenly drawing himself up and adopting a more defensive manner.

'The person I'm interested in learning more about is a Mr Thomas Temple. I don't suppose he's still with you?' asked Lucy hopefully.

'Lady is asking about a Thomas Tinkle,' shouted Stricket.

'Never heard of him,' replied Mincing without looking up from his ledger.

'Thomas Temple,' corrected Lucy.

'Thomas who?' enquired Stricket.

'Thomas Temple,' shouted Lucy, now realising that Stricket was probably as deaf as his partner.

'Thomas Temple?'

'He came from the Foundling Hospital in 1877,' said Lucy, emphasising her words.

'Ah yes, Thomas Temple. I remember Temple,' said Stricket. 'Do you remember young Thomas Temple, Mr Mincing?'

'Thomas Temple? Why yes, Mr Stricket, I remember young Thomas.'

'I don't suppose he's still employed by you?' Lucy asked again.

'What?' shouted Mincing.

'She wants to know whether young Temple is still with us,' said Stricket.

'Oh, he left us many years ago,' replied Mincing, shaking his head.

'Oh dear, I was rather hoping to speak with him,' said a disappointed Lucy. 'How long was he with you?'

'How long was young Temple with us, Mr Mincing?' asked Stricket.

'What? Speak up, Mr Stricket.'

'How long was young Temple with us, Mr Mincing?' repeated Stricket.

'Four years, I believe. We found him very diligent and industrious.'

'So he left in 1881?' suggested Lucy. 'Could you tell me where he went when he left your employment?'

'He didn't leave the company. He went to America,' said Stricket.

'To America!' echoed a surprised Lucy.

'Yes. Our agent in New York, Mr Forester, died unexpectedly, and needed to be replaced, so we sent young Mr Temple there to take his place.'

'What's that you said, Mr Stricket? Forester is dead?' asked a perplexed Mincing.

'Yes, he died in that brawl in that inn. You must remember.'

'Forester dead, you say? Dear me, poor Forester. We'll have to send someone else to replace him,' said Mincing, shaking his head. 'Dear me, this is most unfortunate.'

'So Thomas Temple went to New York as your agent?' asked Lucy, anxious to obtain more information before either of the two partners would forget it. 'What happened to him there? Is he still in New York?'

'We don't know. He worked for us there for a year, or eighteen months, and then we heard nothing else from him,' answered Stricket, shaking his head.

'Temple? We haven't heard from him in a

while,' muttered Mincing.

'So Mr Temple went to New York in 1881 as your agent, and worked there for nearly two years,' repeated Lucy.

'That is so,' said Stricket.

'Have you heard anything from him at all during the past ten years?'

'Nothing at all, I'm afraid,' said Stricket, forcing a brief smile.

'Did he leave a forwarding address?'

'Not as far as I know.'

'And you don't know why he left?'

'No. We wrote, of course, but all our letters were returned. We can only suppose that Mr Temple obtained better employment elsewhere,' suggested Stricket.

'He could have died,' interjected Mincing, much to Lucy's surprise.

'It was all very upsetting at the time. Most unfortunate; he was such a pleasant young fellow,' added Stricket.

'Do you have any photographs, by any chance, of Mr Temple?' asked Lucy.

'No photographs,' answered Stricket.

'What was that?' asked Mincing.

'Lady was asking if we had any photographs of young Mr Temple,' shouted Stricket.

'Oh no, we never took any photographs.'

'I don't suppose you have Mr Temple's

address when he was in New York?' asked Lucy, without any conviction that her question would yield any positive result.

'He boarded at Ma Scrivens' Lodging House in Manhattan,' answered Stricket.

'What's that?' enquired Mincing.

'Young Temple, he resided at Scrivens' Lodging House in Manhattan,' repeated Stricket. 'I remember the name because it was so unusual.'

'So that was where Thomas Temple was living at the time of his disappearance?' asked Lucy.

'Indeed so.'

'Did you write to the lodging house to enquire about Mr Temple's whereabouts?'

'Oh yes, but they never replied,' answered Stricket.

'Well thank you both, Mr Stricket and Mr Mincing. You have been most helpful,' said Lucy, beginning to take her leave.

'We do hope you'll find Mr Temple, Mrs Raven. He was such a pleasant young man. We've often wondered what happened to him,' said Stricket with a smile.

'Thank you once again, gentlemen.'

'Who did she say she was?' asked Mincing.

But Lucy did not hear his reply as she made her way out through the door. As she began to retrace her steps along the narrow alleyway, she suddenly felt a fierce tugging at her coat.

'Lady help?'

She looked down to see that the speaker was the young Chinese girl whom she had encountered prior to her visit to Mincing and Stricket.

'Please, you help,' said the girl, her eyes full of tears as she looked into Lucy's face.

'Whatever is the matter, my dear?'

'Mother, she sick. You must help,' implored the child.

'What's wrong with your mother?' asked a concerned Lucy.

'Mother have accident,' replied the child, tugging harder at Lucy's coat. 'You come. Yes?'

'Well, I don't really know that I should,' said Lucy.

'Mother she is very sick. She die,' said the child, dragging Lucy towards an open door. 'Mother is in there, on floor.'

Lucy strained to peer through the doorway and could just glimpse the sight of a figure lying on the floor inside the building.

'You help?' implored the girl once more, as the figure gave out a pitiful groan.

'Of course,' said Lucy, stepping into the room and walking quickly across towards the injured woman.

Suddenly the door slammed shut behind her. Lucy turned round and found herself surrounded by a group of men. The woman on the floor let out a loud laugh as she jumped to her feet. There was no sign of the girl who had enticed her into the room.

'Don't be afraid,' said one of the men.

Lucy dashed towards the door, but found her way barred by two rough-looking Chinese men. 'I demand you get out of my way,' she protested.

'Missy can't escape,' laughed the man who had spoken first.

'What do you want with me?' asked a frightened Lucy, cursing herself for her own stupidity in entering the room.

'White woman, she fetch a lot,' muttered another of the men.

'Look, I don't know what you want, but I have to tell you that my husband is a police inspector, and that he'll stop at nothing until he's found me,' protested Lucy, feeling very afraid as her words were met by laughter from the group.

'Woman, she worth many pounds,' said the woman who had been lying on the floor.

'Nice coat,' said one of the men, fingering the fabric.

'Get away from me,' shouted Lucy, pushing the man away.

'English woman exchange for much opium,' laughed the first man.

'Look, I'll give you all I have in my purse,' implored Lucy as the group of men closed in on her.

'She mighty fine woman,' grinned one of the men, displaying a set of badly broken teeth.

'Woman get us a good price,' said another, grabbing Lucy by the arm.

'Let go of me,' shouted Lucy as yet more of the men began to pull at her coat.

'You nice woman,' laughed one of the men.

Suddenly the door crashed open, followed by a loud gun shot. Lucy screamed as the men loosened their grip on her and scattered to all sides of the room.

'Quickly — follow me!' shouted the new arrival, grabbing Lucy's arm and pulling her towards the door.

As Lucy burst out the room and into the daylight, she recognised her saviour as the American who had spoken to her on the train.

'Follow me as fast as you can, Mrs Ravenscroft. I have a cab waiting for us around the corner,' said the man, waving his gun in the air. 'Those men are dangerous, and it'll be all up with both of us if they catch us.'

Lucy found herself running faster than she had ever done in her life as she and the

American raced up the alley and round the corner into the street. As she neared a waiting horse-drawn cab, she could hear the sound of distant yells behind her, but feared to look lest her attackers had closed in on them.

'Get into the cab!' yelled the American, throwing open the door. 'Paddington station as fast as you can, and lose those ruffians!' he instructed, following Lucy into the vehicle.

Lucy fought to regain her breath, fearing that her assailants would burst in upon them at any moment. The American flung open the window of the cab and discharged another shot from his gun. Lucy noticed that her hands were shaking.

'We should be all right. They won't catch us now.'

'Thank you,' stuttered Lucy, finding it difficult to speak.

'Don't you worry, Mrs Ravenscroft. They won't trouble us any more,' said her companion, closing the window of the cab and replacing the gun in his pocket. 'You English people, always getting yourselves in trouble.'

'I can't thank you enough.'

'Think nothing of it. But you shouldn't be in this place. Limehouse is worse than Whitechapel, so they say; full of opium dens and houses of ill repute.'

'How do you know my name? Do you know my husband?'

'I know of him, but we've never had the pleasure.'

'What would have happened to me?'

'Oh, they would've sold you to one of the Chinese brothels to feed their opium habit, I have no doubt.'

Lucy covered her face with her hands as she felt tears beginning to form in her eyes.

'Here, lady, now don't you go upsetting yourself,' said the American, handing her a large spotted handkerchief.

'You must think me silly,' said Lucy, dabbing her eyes.

'Don't you worry yourself about that.'

'How did you know I was there?' she asked, trying to recover her composure.

'You English ask a damn lot of silly questions.'

'You were following me?'

'Good thing I was, lady,' he laughed.

'Do you know something about Jacob?'

He banged on the side of the cab. 'Stop here, my man. Take this lady as fast as you can to Paddington station,' he said, handing the man a coin as he stepped down onto the road.

'But wait — what's your name?' protested Lucy.

'My name is immaterial. Go home, Mrs Ravenscroft. You've had a lucky escape. London is no place for a woman on her own. But give your husband a message from me. Tell him that he'd be well advised to give up the case. Nothing good will come of it.'

'But I must thank you — '

'Drive on,' instructed the American, banging on the side of the cab before disappearing from view.

Lucy sat back in the cab, looked down at her still-shaking hands, and found herself living again the terror of the enclosed room.

6

Ledbury

'Well, my dear, I think you've had a very lucky escape,' said Ravenscroft later that evening, after he had listened intently to his wife's adventures in London.

'I was certainly greatly relieved when that American came to my aid. I suppose you're going to reprimand me for going to Limehouse on my own,' said Lucy.

'You did promise that you'd come back straight away after you'd been to the Foundling Hospital,' chided Ravenscroft.

'Yes, I know. But once I'd learnt that young Thomas Temple had left the hospital and gone to Mincing and Stricket, then it seemed only sensible that I should go there and find out what had happened to him. I didn't know that those awful men were going to lure me into that room.'

'I'm only too pleased that no harm came to you. I don't know what the boys and I would have done without you,' said the detective, taking his wife's hand and pressing it to his lips.

'What I can't understand is what that American was doing following me to Limehouse.'

'He is certainly of interest. You say he was already on the train when you got into the compartment here at Ledbury?'

'Yes. The strange thing is that he knew my name, and yet I'm sure I had never met him before, and I certainly never mentioned who I was. Then he wanted to share a cab with me when we arrived at Paddington, which of course I declined. He was obviously following me — but why?'

'He must have an interest in this case, and wanted to see where you were going, and what information you might have obtained about Maria Constantine's son. What did he say again when he left you in the carriage?'

'"Tell your husband that he'd be well advised to give up the case, and that nothing good will come of it,"' replied Lucy, quoting again the American's words.

'What a strange thing to say. Why would I be well advised to give up the case? It almost sounds like a kind of threat to me, but what was he hiding? Do you know, from the description you've given me, I'd say that he very much resembles the man that Mr Lancing saw walking away from his shop just before he discovered that someone had broken in and destroyed all his photographic plates.'

'The same man who took your photographs of Jacob?'

'Yes, and he also made sure that the original photographic plates were also destroyed. I wonder what it is about Jacob that this American didn't want us to know. At present we still don't know whether Maria Constantine's son, Thomas Temple, was actually Jacob. If they *were* both the same man, then that would perhaps explain the American's interest in following you.'

'I wonder what his connection is with Doctor Rockstone.'

'Yes, that is interesting. His accomplice, perhaps.'

'It is not every day that we have two Americans in Ledbury.'

'Indeed. So, let's see what we have. Maria Constantine gives birth to her son in 1862 but gives him up to the Foundling Hospital in London in the hope that he'll have a better life. In 1877 at the age of 15, he's deemed to be of age to make his way in the world, and the hospital authorities apprentice him as a clerk to Mincing and Stricket in Limehouse. Young Thomas obviously does well there, because when their agent in New York dies in some drunken affray, they decide to send

Thomas overseas as their representative. All is well for a while, until one day they hear nothing more from Thomas Temple. I wonder why. Did he die, or did he seek better employment elsewhere? It is all very strange. Then ten years later, Jacob meets up with Rockstone in New York, and they both come over to England, where they join the fair. Now if Thomas Temple did change his name to Jacob, the question is, why did he do that, and also what happened to him between 1882 and now? In my experience, people only change their name because they are running away from something or someone, and are anxious to put the past behind them and start anew.'

'They could still be two different people,' suggested Lucy.

'You could be right. We know that Jacob had a fear of the fair coming to Hereford, so he must have had some kind of unpleasant experience years ago in the county. Thomas Temple, on the other hand, seems to have gone from the Foundling Hospital to Limehouse and then to America. He had no connection with this area, as far as we know. Although his mother came from near here, he was not to know that, so it seems unlikely that he came here, but we cannot say that with any certainty. Maybe he left New York ten years ago, came to Hereford, became involved in something unpleasant, and then went back to New York. It's damn annoying! We're just going round and round in circles. All this is mere speculation.'

'I suppose there have been no sightings of Rockstone?'

'There's been nothing at all. He seems to have gone completely to ground. If only we could find the man, he might be able to provide us with the answers we're looking for,' said Ravenscroft, pouring himself another large drink from the decanter.

'Ma Scrivens' Lodging House, Manhattan!' exclaimed Lucy after a few moments of silence had elapsed.

'Scrivens' Lodging House?' asked Ravenscroft.

'Yes — that's where young Thomas Temple was lodging when he was working for Mincing and Stricket in New York. That's where you should pick up the trail.'

'You're surely not suggesting that I should travel all the way to New York in the hope that I might be able to find out what happened to Thomas?' said Ravenscroft, somewhat taken aback.

'Whyever not? If that's the only way you can solve this case, then that's what you should do,' said Lucy firmly.

'That is ridiculous.'

'It is not ridiculous at all. Why should you not go?'

'Well for a start, New York is a big city, full of many thousands of people. It would be like finding a needle in a haystack. Furthermore, this Scrivens' Lodging House may no longer be in existence; and even if I did manage to locate it, I am sure that young Temple would have left there long ago, and then what would I do?'

'Well, you would ask around and find out what had happened to him, like you usually do,' said an excited Lucy.

'No, no, this is quite impossible,' protested Ravenscroft.

'You — we — owe it to Maria Constantine. I'm sure you'd want to reunite her with her son, if there's any chance that he's still alive.'

'The superintendent would never countenance my sailing off to New York.'

'You don't know until you ask him. If it's the only way this case can be solved, then you should go.'

'But I couldn't leave you and the children on your own.'

'Why not? We can take care of ourselves. I promise I won't be going back to Limehouse ever again. I'm sure you wouldn't be away for very long.'

'New York is on the other side of the world.'

'There are ships that go from Liverpool.'

'I couldn't leave the investigation here.'

'Tom is more than capable of taking charge of the search for Rockstone.'

'Yes, I suppose you're right on that count.'

'Then you have no more excuses not to go,' said Lucy, with a degree of triumph in her voice.

'I'll give it some thought,' mumbled Ravenscroft.

'In the meantime, I think I should write to Miss Constantine and tell her what I've discovered about her son.'

'I don't think you should get her hopes up, my dear.'

'It is the least I can do. I promised we would help her. Samuel, you must go to New York. You must see that it's the only hope you have of solving this case.'

'We'll have to see what the superintendent has to say about it.'

★　★　★

'Come in!' boomed a familiar voice from the other side of the door.

Ravenscroft coughed before entering the room. A large overdressed figure sporting a red carnation waved a hand in the direction of a chair placed before the desk. Ravenscroft advanced hesitantly before sitting on the seat and looking around the drab room with its book-lined shelves and faded photographs.

'Be with you in a minute, Ravenscroft; just fixing this little beauty into position,' said the superintendent, head bent downwards, eyes focused closely on the open glass case before him. 'There we are; the Silver Studded Blue Butterfly. She looks a beauty; been after her for years. You collect butterflies, Ravenscroft?'

'No, sir.'

'You should do so. Rewarding hobby; gives one an interest outside the force. Teaches one all about the world, as well as relaxing the mind,' said his superior, looking up as he closed the lid of the case.

'I'm afraid I've never had the time or the inclination.'

'Damn poor show I call that,' muttered his superior, giving him a look of disapproval. 'Well what can I do for you, Ravenscroft?'

'It's the Jacob case, sir.'

'Yes, been reading your report,' said the superintendent, sitting down in his large office chair and tapping a folder on his desk.

Ravenscroft thought it best not to say anything.

'Not making much progress, are we?'

'I'm afraid not, sir.'

'Still haven't caught this Rockstain fellow.'

'Rockstone, sir,' corrected Ravenscroft.

'Yes, yes, Rockstain, Rockstone, whatever his name. We can't have these loose Americans causing havoc over here and then disappearing.'

'No, sir, but I can assure you that we're doing our best to apprehend this man.'

'Got to find him first,' said the superintendent sarcastically.

'Yes, sir,' replied a somewhat deflated Ravenscroft.

'Now you want to go halfway round the world to New York, of all places.'

'Yes.'

'Well I'm afraid it just won't do. It won't do at all. It's totally out of the question.'

'It may be the only way we can solve this case, sir. If I can find the whereabouts of this Thomas Temple in New York, I may be able to find out who murdered Jacob,' said Ravenscroft, realising that he was probably not going to succeed with his request.

'The word is 'may', as you say.'

'If I don't try, I fear this will go down in our archives as an unsolved case.'

'Don't like unsolved crimes; bad for morale,' replied the superintendent, tapping his fingers on the folder.

'Precisely, sir.'

'No, no, it just won't do. Sending one of my officers to the other side of the world on some wild goose chase will never do. The budget won't stand it; and if you go, who's going to run things in Ledbury and continue the search for this Rockstone person?'

'Constable Crabb is very able, sir. He's been with me for over four years now, and during all that time I've found him most industrious and diligent.'

'That's as may be,' replied Ravenscroft's superior, showing signs of irritation. 'But it just won't do. We can't afford the expense, and that's an end to the matter.'

'I believe I have some leave due, sir,' said Ravenscroft, deciding to change course.

'I suppose you have.'

'Then if I chose to go to New York at my own expense, and in my own time, I trust you'd have no objection; and as I've just said, Crabb is more than capable of continuing the case over here during my absence.'

'I don't know, Ravenscroft. If it ever got out that I sent one of my officers all the way to New York, we could be made to look very foolish. I'm still very unhappy about all of this.'

Ravenscroft looked disappointedly down at the floor.

'Sorry, Ravenscroft. I know you've put a

great deal of effort into the solving of this case, but I cannot permit such an enterprise.'

'Very well, sir,' said a dejected Ravenscroft.

'See yourself out, won't you.'

'Butterflies!' exclaimed Ravenscroft suddenly, an idea coming into his mind.

'Butterflies? What about butterflies?'

'I understand that there are some rather rare butterflies to be found in America?'

'That is correct.'

'Well, sir, perhaps if I could locate one or two dealers of butterflies registered in New York, I could perhaps bring back one or two specimens,' suggested Ravenscroft, realising that his request might be about to take a more positive direction.

'Excellent suggestion, Ravenscroft! What a capital idea! You should have mentioned it earlier.'

'Then you'd have no further objections if I went in my own time, as I have just said?'

'Absolutely!' said the superintendent, rising from his desk. 'Marvellous. But you must let me contribute to the cost of your fare. Where are you sailing from?'

'There's a Cunard ship leaving Liverpool the day after tomorrow; the *Etruria*,' replied Ravenscroft. 'And I'll accept your most generous offer, if I may. I'll see what I can bring back with me.'

'That's wonderful news, Ravenscroft. I'll just give you the names of one or two North American butterflies that I am especially keen to acquire. Capital.'

'Oh, and just before I go, sir — I wonder if I might have a word with you about another pressing matter?'

★ ★ ★

The following morning found Ravenscroft and Lucy conversing with one another on the platform of Ledbury station, with Crabb standing discreetly a few feet away.

'Now, my dear, you must promise me that you won't be going off on any more of your adventures to London, or elsewhere, during my absence,' said Ravenscroft.

'I give you my word, Samuel. Now do stop worrying. The boys and I will be just fine,' replied Lucy, adjusting her husband's tie and brushing away a hair from the top of his coat.

'I should be back within two to three weeks. The crossing is usually seven or eight days, and I don't intend to stay in New York for longer that I have to.'

'You must remain there as long as you consider necessary. I've packed your case with everything I think you'll need. I've also taken the liberty of including some reading material for the voyage, should you find yourself becoming bored.' Lucy smiled.

'Sherlock Holmes?' asked Ravenscroft hopefully.

'*Barchester Towers*. Anthony Trollope. It's quite long, but not as long as some of his other novels; and yes, I did find you the latest edition of the *Strand Magazine*, which has another story by Mr Conan Doyle.'

'Excellent.'

'And if you get bored, you can always start writing your memoirs.'

'I don't think so.'

'And make sure you wrap up well on that ship, as it is bound to be quite cold and windy,' instructed Lucy. 'I've heard that the Atlantic can often be a rough crossing at this time of year.'

'Of course I will, my dear. I am going to miss you frightfully. I rather wish I wasn't going now.'

'Now Samuel, you know that we must do all that we can to help Miss Constantine. I gave her my word that we would do everything we could to find her son.'

'Yes, I know.'

'Just make sure that you come back to us.'

'Of course.'

'I think I can hear the train approaching.'

'I'd better have a word with Tom,' said

Ravenscroft, walking across towards the constable.

'I wish you well with your travels, sir,' said Crabb.

'Thank you. You have my full authority to act on your own initiative during my absence. I'm sure you'll manage quite well. If you apprehend Rockstone, make sure you question him and try and get a confession out of him; and if he killed Jacob, I want to know why.'

'Yes, sir.'

'I have every faith in you, Tom.'

'Thank you.'

'Oh yes, and make sure we know where the travelling fair is going during the next two months or so, should we need to go back and question Walker and his associates further,' shouted Ravenscroft above the noise of the steam train as it pulled into the station.

'Yes, sir.'

'Goodbye, my dear,' Ravenscroft said to Lucy. He added, turning to Crabb, 'All the best with the investigation, Tom,' before opening the carriage door.

'Take care, Samuel; come back safely to us,' cried out an anxious Lucy.

'Good luck, sir,' added Crabb, assisting Ravenscroft with his case into the compartment.

'I won't be long,' shouted out the detective as the train began to pull out of the station.

Lucy and Crabb waved back at the outstretched hand, then watched in silence as the train turned the corner and disappeared from view. 'Well, Tom, it looks as though we're on our own now,' said the former.

'Indeed so, Mrs Ravenscroft. But I'm sure it won't be long before the inspector safely returns.'

'I hope so, Tom. I hope so.'

7

At Sea

Ravenscroft flung down the book onto the hard and uncomfortable bunk and gave out a deep sigh.

The *Etruria* had left Liverpool three days earlier, and although the sea had been relatively calm at the time of its departure, by the end of the next day a violent storm had driven its passengers, Ravenscroft among them, to seek the sanctuary of their cabins.

At first Ravenscroft had almost welcomed the opportunity of retreating to his simply furnished single second-class cabin; but having long exhausted the contents of the latest edition of the *Strand Magazine*, and finding that the Proudies and Hardings of Barchester were something that he could not quite take to, he had begun to tire of the confines of the little room with its continual pitching back and forth and its creaking boards, and longed for a calmer sea and a tranquil voyage so that he might stretch his legs once more.

Lying on his bed, he found his mind

turning again to the case in hand. Quite why he had agreed to embark on this adventure to a strange country, he could not be sure. He told himself that even if he did find the lodging house where the young Thomas Temple had boarded over ten years ago, there was still no guarantee that the man would still be there; and if he had left the residence, it would surely be doubtful whether anyone could remember him, or know where he had gone. New York was apparently quite a large city, and the inspector knew this task could be like searching for a needle in a haystack. Furthermore, if Temple had travelled to another part of America, or returned to England, or gone to anywhere else in the world, then the search would prove almost impossible.

Ravenscroft told himself that even if he were fortunate in his quest to find Temple, that at least would prove he was not the man known as Jacob, and he would then be able to reunite Maria Constantine with her son. But then he reminded himself that if he found Temple, perhaps the man might not wish to abandon the life he had created for himself in the new world for the sake of a mother who had abandoned him when he had been only an infant. It might even be better if he could establish that Temple and Jacob were one and the same person. At least that way he might be able to discover who had killed Jacob and why — then he would be able to solve the crime; but even that hope now seemed a remote possibility.

No, it had been foolish to even think that this mad adventure could yield anything of value. He should have remained in Ledbury and carried on the search for Rockstone. He was still convinced that it was the travelling quack doctor who held the key to this mystery. He cursed himself for his folly.

A loud knock on his cabin door broke into his deliberations. 'Good evening, sir,' said the cheery steward, opening the door.

'Evening already?' asked Ravenscroft, rising from his bed.

'Six o'clock, sir. You'll be pleased to know that the storm has abated.'

'Thank goodness. Does that mean I can now go up onto the deck?' asked Ravenscroft hopefully.

'Indeed, sir.'

'Then that is good news.'

'Can I assist you with your coat?' said the steward with a smile.

'That is most kind of you.'

A few minutes later after climbing, with difficulty, up two flights of steps, Ravenscroft found himself on the promenade deck of the vessel. Although the steward had claimed that the storm had ended, Ravenscroft was not so sure of that assertion; and as he clung to the rail at the side of the deck in an attempt to prevent the wind from blowing him elsewhere, he looked out across the huge waves that crashed into the side of the ship. As he attempted to clear his spectacles from the spray that covered the lenses, the detective began to wish that he had remained in the landlocked town of Ledbury, and cursed the folly of his decision to sail across the unpleasant ocean.

'You get used to it after a while.'

Ravenscroft turned to find that he had been joined by a tall grey-haired elderly gentleman dressed in a thick astrakhan overcoat and fur hat. 'I don't think that will ever be the case,' he replied.

'Oh, when you've made the crossing a few times, you kind of get used to all the wind and rain,' continued the man, speaking in what Ravenscroft identified as an American accent.

'I only intend to make this one crossing and the return journey,' said the inspector. 'I have no inclination to set sail ever again.'

'You say that now, but I can assure you that once the sun is out tomorrow and the sea is calm, it will seem like a different world out here,' said the man with a smile.

'You know that tomorrow will be different?'

asked Ravenscroft hopefully.

'I believe so, but then again I could be wrong.'

'You make this crossing a great deal?'

'Generally two or three times a year. I try and avoid the winter months. It can be quite cold and icy in New York in January and February.'

'So I believe. I'm glad it's October.'

'Can get rather foggy now, but you shouldn't encounter many problems. So this will be your first visit to our fine city?'

'Indeed.'

'I take it your visit is one based on business rather than pleasure, my dear sir?'

'Your assumption is correct.'

'Sorry, we haven't been introduced, and I know you English like your formalities. My name is William O'Callaghan. I'm in the export and import business.'

'Samuel Ravenscroft.'

'And what line of business brings you to New York, Mr Ravenscroft?'

'Butterflies,' replied Ravenscroft, not wanting to give away his true occupation to the stranger.

'Butterflies!' exclaimed the American. 'Well I'll be darned. You're coming all this way for butterflies?'

'Yes, I believe there are some rather rare

139

butterflies in North America. I hope to acquire some specimens for myself and my friends, to add to our collections,' answered Ravenscroft, regretting that he had been so forthcoming on a subject about which he knew so little, and fearing that he might be caught out by the stranger at any moment.

'Well I've heard it all now. I know you English collect fine furniture, paintings and other bygone relics, but it's the first time I've ever met anyone who collects butterflies. You English eccentrics, that's what I like about you,' said the American, giving out a hearty laugh.

'You say your name is O'Callaghan?' asked Ravenscroft, quickly seeking to turn the conversation in another direction, but wishing that the loud man would go away.

'My grandfather was Irish, as you can probably tell by my name. He came from a little village in County Kerry. Then he fell on hard times and took his family off to America to seek a better life — and do you know, he found it there. America really is a land of opportunity. I was born in New York, so I can say that I'm a hundred percent American, and proud of it as well.'

'I'm sure you are. May I ask what you export and import?'

'Confidential, my friend,' replied the

American defensively as he stared sternly at Ravenscroft.

'I am sorry, I did not wish to pry,' said Ravenscroft, realising that he might have caused some offence with his question.

'I know. You English, always wanting to know what we old colonials are up to,' laughed the American, quickly reverting to his former way of speaking. 'See here — I think you and I, Mr Ravenscroft, are going to get along with each other just fine. Why don't you have dinner with me tomorrow evening, and you can tell me more about those quaint old butterflies you're so interested in.'

'I wouldn't wish to intrude.'

'No intrusion, my dear sir, I can assure you.'

'Well, that is most kind of you, Mr O'Callaghan.'

'Good, that's settled then. See you at seven tomorrow evening, in the first-class dining room?'

'I'm afraid I am only travelling second class,' said Ravenscroft, hoping that this excuse would prove sufficient for the invitation to be rescinded.

'No problem. I'll have a word with the head waiter. Now if you'll excuse me, I think I've had enough of this Atlantic air for one night.'

'Goodnight, Mr O'Callaghan.'

Ravenscroft watched as the American made

his way along the deck and in through one of the doors, wondering what had possessed him to accept a dinner invitation from a man whom he scarcely knew, and whom he did not particularly like.

★ ★ ★

The next day the sun did indeed shine, and Ravenscroft took the opportunity of walking up and down the promenade deck in the morning before acquiring one of the deck chairs at the quieter end of the vessel, which also afforded some shelter from the wind.

After lunch he visited the ship's library and asked the librarian there whether the collection included any books on butterflies, and was somewhat relieved when the man took down a large volume from one of the shelves. Ravenscroft then retired to a corner of the saloon, where he spent the remainder of the afternoon turning over its pages and attempting to memorize the names of those butterflies that were known to be resident species of North America.

It was a rather hesitant Ravenscroft who entered the first-class dining room just after seven that evening. As he gave his name to the head waiter at the door, he hoped that even now he would be refused admittance;

but it appeared that the man knew of his impending arrival and escorted him to a corner of the room, where he found his host already in residence.

'Ah, Ravenscroft, glad you could come. May I introduce you to my two fellow travellers, Mr Petters and Mr Foy,' said the American, standing up from the table.

'Good evening, gentlemen,' said Ravenscroft, observing that whereas the first gentleman was of an overweight and red-faced appearance, his companion was of a thin, nervous disposition.

'Come, don't wait on ceremony,' said O'Callaghan, indicating that Ravenscroft should occupy the remaining seat.

'Thank you.'

'Mr Ravenscroft here is a collector of butterflies; and would you believe it, he's travelling all the way across to New York in the hope of adding to his collection.'

'Yes indeed,' replied Ravenscroft somewhat apprehensively.

'I had an uncle who once collected buttons,' said Petters.

'Buttons!' exclaimed O'Callaghan. 'What the heck would anyone want from collecting something as dull as buttons?'

'He didn't think they were dull,' retorted Petters.

'And what do you collect, Mr Foy?' asked Ravenscroft, saying the first thing that came into his head.

Foy said nothing as he stared at Ravenscroft, giving a slight twitch on the left side of his face as he did so.

'You must excuse our friend Mr Foy. He is a man of few words. Isn't that so, Foy?' said O'Callaghan, touching his friend on the shoulder.

'If you say so,' muttered Foy with another twitch of his face before he looked vacantly into the distance.

'Now what would you like, Ravenscroft?' said his host as the waiter handed the detective a large menu.

'Wish this voyage would soon be over,' grumbled Foy as Ravenscroft studied the menu.

'Mr Foy is not a good traveller, are you, Foy? I think he prefers a horse,' laughed O'Callaghan.

Ravenscroft observed that Foy gave another twitch of his face before turning away in some annoyance.

'Now, Ravenscroft, tell us more about these butterflies of yours. I'm sure that my colleagues, Mr Petters and Mr Foy, would be most interested to learn more about your great hobby,' urged O'Callaghan, looking intently at the detective as a waiter lit a large cigar for him.

'Well, I . . . er . . . I haven't been collecting them for very long,' replied Ravenscroft, before going on to name a number of butterflies he had found in the book he had borrowed earlier from the library, and hoping that he would not be found out by any of his dining companions.

'Seems you know quite a lot about your subject. But where do you put all these dead butterflies?' asked O'Callaghan.

'Oh, I mount them on card and put them in trays in a cabinet,' replied Ravenscroft, remembering his superior's collection back in Worcester.

'And which butterflies do you wish to acquire in New York?' asked O'Callaghan, staring intently at Ravenscroft before puffing on his cigar.

The detective struggled to remember the names of several of the creatures his superior had mentioned to him before leaving England.

'Well, that's pretty impressive, is it not, gentlemen?' said O'Callaghan, turning towards his two companions.

'Very,' remarked Petters without enthusiasm as he poured himself another glass of wine. Foy gave a sigh and twitched once more.

'And where do you hope to acquire these butterflies, Mr Ravenscroft?' asked O'Callaghan.

'I believe there are one or two dealers in butterflies in New York.'

'Well I'll be darned. Who would have thought there were dealers in New York selling that kind of thing?' laughed O'Callaghan. 'We'll have to see if we can assist Mr Ravenscroft in his search, will we not, Mr Petters?'

'Indeed,' replied a disinterested Petters.

★ ★ ★

Two hours later, a somewhat relieved Ravenscroft sought the quiet sanctuary of his cabin. He had found the dinner a somewhat daunting experience. Petters had been particularly blunt in his answers, almost to the point of rudeness, whereas his companion Foy had said so little during the evening that Ravenscroft had found it difficult to avert his gaze from the man's uncontrollable twitching.

But it had been O'Callaghan's continual questioning and accompanying stare that had unsettled him the most. He had done his best not to give away either his true occupation or the real reason for his visit to New York, whilst trying to pass himself off as an eccentric English butterfly collector; but as the evening had progressed, Ravenscroft had become gradually aware that perhaps his dining companions had begun to see through the façade he had created. Then there had been the large waves of smoke from the American's cigar, which had drifted irritatingly across the table in his direction; the loudness of his host's boisterous conversation; and the particularly aggressive manner in which Petters ate his food, which had all added to the unpleasantness of the evening.

Ravenscroft had formed a great dislike of the three men. He had met Americans before during his long years in Whitechapel, some of whom had been outgoing and untrustworthy in their nature. Some had been violent; one or two had even been arrested for murder. But these men were different. Something told him that these Americans were not to be trusted, and that any future contact with them was fraught with possible danger.

As Ravenscroft undressed and retired to his bed, he resolved to avoid any future contact with the three men for the remainder of the voyage.

★ ★ ★

After an unsettled night, during which he had dreamt of large swarms of butterflies circling

147

and attacking him in a large field, and had awoken several times and found himself lying in a cold sweat, Ravenscroft climbed out of his bed and made his way across the room to the water jug to relieve his dry throat. As he poured himself some water into a glass, he observed that a note had been pushed underneath the door of his cabin. He bent down, picked up the paper, and read its contents:

Keep away from O'Callaghan. He is not
    to be trusted.
He is a dangerous man.
Believe me when I say that I have your
    best interests at heart.
A friend.

Ravenscroft read the note several times and examined the large untidy hand in which it had been written. Who could possibly have penned such a letter? He had not made the acquaintance of anyone else on the ship, so it seemed unlikely that this so-called 'friend' could have been known to him. It was also unlikely that either of O'Callaghan's companions, Petters or Foy, would have sent the message. Why was he now being warned against the American? He certainly did not like the group and wished he had never dined with them, but he had to remind himself that although he distrusted them, his dislike of them did not necessarily make them criminals.

Then Ravenscroft remembered the words that Lucy's saviour had uttered when he had left her cab: 'Tell your husband he would be well advised to give up the case; he would do well to leave things alone.' He wondered whether this new message could also have been written by the same person. If so, why had this man warned him against following up the Jacob case, as well as now advising him to keep away from O'Callaghan and his associates? Had the three Americans something to do with Jacob's murder? Perhaps Thomas Temple had also been known to these men.

Ravenscroft knew that he did not have the answers to these questions, but he now realised that there were others on the ship intent on taking a keen personal interest in his activities. He was also conscious that he was about to enter a new country where he would be very much on his own; where there would be no Crabb or any other police colleagues he would be able to call upon should he be in need of them. He knew that he would need to be even more diligent than usual, and remain on his guard against anything or anyone that might prevent him from learning the truth.

* * *

The remainder of the voyage seemed to Ravenscroft to pass quite quickly, and by keeping very much to himself he was able to avoid any further contact with the three Americans. On the final day, he made his way out onto the deck. The early-morning mist was already beginning to clear, and the gradual appearance of a number of buildings in the distance was a welcoming sight after so many days at sea. Ravenscroft knew it would not be long before he could disembark and make his way to Ma Scrivens' Lodging House, where hopefully he could begin his investigations.

He returned to his cabin as the ship pulled into the harbour side and other passengers began to gather on the decks, as he had no desire to encounter O'Callaghan and his two associates during his departure. After a few minutes had elapsed he tipped his cabin steward, and carrying his suitcase made his way down to the gangplank, glad to feel once again the reassuring steadiness of land. He joined the throng of passengers on the quay side, and after completing the required formalities he made his way through a large building and out into the open air, where he observed a line of cabs waiting to take the new arrivals into the city.

'Ravenscroft — jump up here and I'll give you a lift,' shouted out a familiar voice from the inside of a cab that drew up suddenly in front of him.

'I think I will be fine, thank you,' he replied, realising that the speaker was O'Callaghan.

'That's nonsense, man. Where are you headed?'

'Scrivens' Lodging House,' replied Ravenscroft somewhat hesitantly.

'I'm going the same way. Get in,' said the American, throwing open the door with some force so that it almost hit Ravenscroft in the face.

'I am sure it's an inconvenience,' stuttered Ravenscroft, hoping that O'Callaghan might yet rescind his invitation and he could avoid any further contact with the man.

'Not at all. You'll have the devil of a wait over there. Don't stand on ceremony. Get in, man.'

Ravenscroft reluctantly stepped into the cab, which he found occupied by O'Callaghan and Foy. 'You English, always so darned reticent,' said the former.

'That is most kind of you,' replied a somewhat nervous Ravenscroft.

'Staying at Ma Scrivens' then?' asked O'Callaghan.

'Yes, it was recommended to me by a friend.'

'Do you hear that, Foy? Our English friend here says that Ma Scrivens' was recommended to him by a friend,' laughed O'Callaghan out loud.

'Really,' said Foy sourly with a twitch of his face.

'God, man, you don't want to stay at that dreadful forsaken place. You won't last two days there. Look, why don't you stay at my hotel?'

'That's very kind of you, but I feel I must decline. I have already made a reservation,' protested Ravenscroft, a sickening feeling in his stomach.

'Well you can cancel it. You come and stay with us.'

'No, really, I can't.'

'Whyever not, man?'

'I'm meeting a friend of mine who's already staying there,' said Ravenscroft, thinking as quickly as he could to come up with some excuse.

'Well if you must. What do you think of New York so far?'

'It seems very noisy and busy,' replied the inspector, looking out of the window of the cab.

'Yep, there is sure plenty going on here.

We're always on the move; building every-where. We'll soon run out of space; then I guess we'll just have to build upwards into the sky.'

Ravenscroft gave a brief smile as he continued to watch the sights of the city as the cab made its way along the busy streets.

'I tell you Ravenscroft, London ain't got nothing on this place.'

'No, I suppose not.'

A few minutes later the cab turned down a narrow road, eventually stopping outside a large five-storey building situated at the corner of two streets.

'That's Ma Scrivens'. If you don't like the look of it, my offer still stands,' said O'Callaghan, leaning forwards and breathing closely into Ravenscroft's face.

'No, it will be fine,' replied the detective, beginning to alight from the cab.

'See here, Ravenscroft — you just take my card. It has the name of my hotel on it. Feel free to come and join us any time you like,' urged O'Callaghan, thrusting the item into Ravenscroft's hand.

'Thank you for the ride,' said the detective, taking the card and closing the cab door behind him.

'Be seeing you!' shouted the American as the cab sped off in a cloud of dust.

Ravenscroft let out a deep sigh of relief and looked up at the tall building. For a moment he thought he had stepped backwards in time; for the drab, untidy structure, with its peeling paint, damaged rusty wrought-iron balconies and decaying woodwork reminded him of some of the most notorious slums he had experienced during his police days in Whitechapel. A board bearing the name 'Scrivens' Lodging House' hung crookedly over the entrance door, and a smell of smoke and decaying rubbish seemed to hang over the whole neighbourhood. Perhaps it had been unwise to contemplate staying in such a residence, but Ravenscroft told himself that if he was to discover what had happened to Thomas Temple, then he would have to put any reservations he had about the lodging house to one side. At least he had managed to escape from the overbearing O'Callaghan and his associate.

Ravenscroft pushed open the door and found that he was now facing a large wooden counter at the end of a passageway, behind which stood an elderly man with a long flowing beard, wearing untidy clothes and lopsided wire spectacles.

'Good morning. I would like a room please,' said Ravenscroft.

'You ain't from around these parts, then?'

enquired the man without looking up from the book he had been reading.

'England,' replied Ravenscroft, placing his case on the floor. 'I've just disembarked from the *Etruria*.'

'What do you want a room for?' said the man, looking up and staring hard at Ravenscroft.

'I was under the impression that this was a lodging house, and anyway I have nowhere else to stay.'

'How long?'

'Pardon?'

'How long do you want to stay for?'

'For two or three days; I am not quite sure at the moment.'

The man stared again intently at Ravenscroft for a few seconds without saying anything, before suddenly calling out, 'Ma!' Ravenscroft shuffled his feet as the man repeated the call, without success.

'Look, surely you can give me a room,' protested the inspector, finding that the man's inhospitable manner was beginning to annoy him.

The man yelled the same command for a third time. Suddenly a door to the left of the counter sprang open. 'What do you want?' shouted a tall, red, sweaty-faced, heavily built woman entering the room.

'Gent here wants a room, Ma. He says he's from England. Just got off one of them boats,' said the old man.

'Does he? Why has he come here?' replied the woman in an aggressive tone, addressing her question to the man rather than to Ravenscroft himself.

'Your establishment was recommended to me,' interjected Ravenscroft.

The man gave out a hearty laugh.

'Who by?' asked the woman.

'You were recommended by a friend of mine in England who once lodged with you here.'

'Did he? That's as may be,' said the woman in a dismissive tone.

'Look, is this house a boarding establishment or is it not?' asked an irritated Ravenscroft, raising his voice.

'It is.'

'So you have rooms? I would be obliged if I can have one of them.'

'Put him in number five,' replied the woman before turning her back and exiting quickly through the door.

The clerk opened a large ledger. 'Sign here.' He indicated the place with a dirty brown withered finger.

Ravenscroft entered his name. 'I presume that was Ma Scrivens?' he asked.

'Yep,' replied the clerk, banging the ledger to with a bang. 'That'll be ten dollars in advance. Dinner is at seven.'

Ravenscroft handed over the money. The man resumed his writing.

'Could you tell me where number five is?' asked Ravenscroft after a moment's silence had elapsed, during which time he realised that the man did not seem inclined to either show him the way or carry his case for him to his new abode.

'Up the stairs, turn right, up the stairs, turn left, up the stairs, third door on the right,' replied the man after giving out a loud sigh.

'Thank you,' said Ravenscroft, picking up his case.

'You need that,' said the man, banging a large key on the counter before turning on his heel and walking out of the side door.

Ravenscroft picked up the key and began to make his way up the first flight of stairs. Pausing only to look at the peeling walls and threadbare carpet on the first landing, he then continued to follow the clerk's instructions and began the ascent of the second narrower flight of stairs. Upon reaching the next landing, he rested for a moment to ease his congested lungs before proceeding upwards onto the third landing, where he located the third door on the right, which bore a faded sign indicating that he had at last reached the end of his journey.

Opening the creaking door, Ravenscroft entered and looked round the simply furnished room, which consisted of a brass bedstead, wooden wardrobe and chair, and side table upon which stood a chipped jug and bowel. A faded coloured print of the Virgin Mary hung crookedly from one of the walls, and he observed that the hue of the bed cover was of a dubious nature.

Placing his case on the floor and removing his coat, Ravenscroft crossed over to the window and strained to peer through the dirt-stained pane. Opposite him was a building of similar structure and height that appeared to be in no better condition than the house he had just entered, and to either side of it the view extended over crowded streets and houses, stretching forever into the distance. Black clouds of smoke rising from numerous factories drifted across the city, and although it was only midday it seemed more like early evening.

Ravenscroft reached into his coat pocket, took out the locket, and gazed at the portrait inside before casting another glance round the miserable room. He wondered whether this had been the actual room where Temple had lodged upon his arrival in America. If so, that might explain why the young man had one day left it all behind him.

Ravenscroft wondered whether he had perhaps been foolish to have left Ledbury and to have undertaken such a long journey halfway round the world on what might well prove to be but a futile quest. Would he be able to find out what had happened to Thomas Temple all those years ago? And furthermore, if he did eventually track down the missing man, would that then enable him to finally discover who had murdered Jacob — or would his investigations lead to nothing?

Feelings of apprehension and despair suddenly seemed to overwhelm him as he felt the utter loneliness of his present situation. Throwing himself down on the bed with a deep sigh, he looked up at the large damp patch on the ceiling above him and resolved that he would endeavour to make his stay in the metropolis as short as possible.

8

The Orchards

Lucy closed the door of the cottage behind her and walked down the cobbled street to the marketplace in Ledbury.

On the day after her husband's departure for New York, she had written a letter to Maria Constantine detailing her experiences in London, and telling her of how her son had fared at the Foundling Hospital, and then at Mincing and Stricket, before his departure for America. She had ended with the news of Ravenscroft's journey to the New World. Earlier that day she had received a reply in which Maria had expressed both her gratitude and her hopes for the future. Now Lucy's thoughts turned once more to the event on Hangman Hill.

'Good morning, Tom,' she said as she entered the tiny police station in Ledbury.

'Good morning, Mrs Ravenscroft,' replied the young policeman with a smile.

'I was just passing, so I thought I would see how the investigation is progressing.'

'Not as well I would have hoped. In fact we

have had no luck at all in catching the elusive Doctor Rockstone. He seems to have vanished into thin air. I wouldn't be surprised if he's gone back to America.'

'Never mind,' sympathised Lucy.

'Perhaps Mr Ravenscroft will have better fortune with his enquiries in New York. He should have arrived by now.'

'Indeed,' answered Lucy. 'Tom, I've been thinking a great deal about this case. Why do you think Jacob was hung from a tree on the top of Hangman Hill?'

'I've just been asking myself the same question, Mrs Ravenscroft. It does seem rather odd. They could have hung the fellow from any tree.'

'Yes, so why was he killed there of all places? It's as though the hill had some significance for whoever committed the crime.'

'Something terrible could have happened there all those years ago,' suggested Crabb.

'Exactly. But whatever took place there must have happened before either you or I came to the area, or we would have known about it.'

'Those were my thoughts entirely.'

'So how can we find out about the hill and what might have happened there?'

'I know just the person who might be able

161

to answer that question,' answered Crabb enthusiastically. 'If I saddle the horse and trap, would you care to accompany me to Malvern, Mrs Ravenscroft?'

'Yes indeed, Tom.'

★ ★ ★

Later that morning Lucy and Crabb made their way along Belle Vue Terrace in Malvern, until they reached the Malvern Library and Reading Rooms at the corner of the road.

'Good morning, madam — and Constable Crabb again, if I am not mistaken,' said Clifford the librarian as they entered the building.

'Good morning to you, Mr Clifford. May I introduce you to Mrs Ravenscroft,' said Crabb.

'I am delighted to make your acquaintance, Mrs Ravenscroft.'

'Good morning to you, Mr Clifford,' said Lucy with a smile. 'I have heard so much about you and your excellent library.'

'The good inspector is not with you this morning?'

'He is away on business,' replied Lucy, not wanting to give too much information away regarding her husband's activities.

'Then how can I be of assistance to you?'

'It is regarding the death of that man on Hangman Hill,' said Crabb.

'Ah yes.'

'We were wondering whether anything else of a tragic nature has ever occurred on that hill,' asked Lucy.

'Not as far as I'm aware. Of course I have only been here in Malvern for the past seven years,' replied Clifford in his usual polite and formal manner.

'This event could have happened ten or more years ago,' suggested Crabb.

'We thought that you might have some records that we could examine,' added Lucy.

'If something of a serious nature did occur on the hill, then it would have been recorded in the *Malvern News*. We do have back copies of the newspaper here, but it would take a great deal of time to go through them.'

'Then perhaps we should make a start, Mr Clifford,' said Crabb.

'Of course. If you would both care to follow me into the other room,' said Clifford, leading the way.

Lucy and Crabb entered the inner room, which was lined with volumes of books and newspapers. 'The newspaper was bound in volumes, and each volume contains approximately three months of weekly issues. Where would you like to start?' asked Clifford. Lucy

163

and Crabb looked at one another. 'Perhaps I might suggest that you commence with 1880 and work forwards until say, 1884; and then if we do not find anything there, we would have to go back further in time.'

'That would be most acceptable,' said Lucy, taking the chair that the librarian offered.

Clifford bought over two large volumes and gave one each to Crabb and Lucy. 'I am afraid I must leave you to your task, as I have one or two other customers I must see to in the lounge. You will find the other volumes clearly marked on the shelves behind you.'

'Thank you, Mr Clifford,' said Lucy.

'I wish you well with your search,' Clifford said with a smile before leaving the room.

'Well, we'd better make a start,' said Lucy, opening the large volume.

During the next hour, both Lucy and Crabb turned over the weekly pages of the *Malvern News*, twice replacing the volumes that had been selected by the librarian.

'I think we have it, Tom!' exclaimed Lucy.

Crabb stood up and looked over her shoulder as she read from the volume:

TRAGEDY ON THE HILLS.
YOUNG GIRL FOUND DEAD ON
HANGMAN HILL.

The body of a young woman was recovered last Monday evening from the summit of Hangman Hill in the Malvern Hills.

It is understood that the deceased, Lizzie Warren, was employed as a milk-maid at Orchard Farm, Parkway, near Ledbury, Herefordshire, and had been out walking on the hills when she fell and sustained a fatal injury. The incident has been reported to the local constabulary in Malvern, but our reporter has been informed by Inspector Robinson that no foul play has been suspected.

'Well it seems that we were right, Mrs Ravenscroft; something terrible did happen on that hill all those years ago,' said Crabb.

'The poor girl; how unfortunate. Tom, do you think we can find out anything else about this case?' asked Lucy.

'There could be a police file. I'll make enquiries.'

'I wonder if there were any further reports in the newspaper,' said Lucy, turning over the pages. 'Yes, here we are. There are just a few lines giving news of the inquest. 'Death caused by misadventure. Tragic accident.' There must be a connection between the death of this poor woman and Jacob.'

'I remember that the police inspector in Malvern, before I arrived, was a certain Alfred Robinson. According to the newspaper report, it seems that he was investigating the case. He lives in a small cottage on The Green in Colwall. I think we should pay him a visit. He may be able to tell us more about the case,' suggested Crabb.

'I think that's an excellent idea, Tom.'

★　★　★

A few minutes later, Crabb pulled up the horse outside a small brick-built cottage situated on The Green in the Herefordshire village of Colwall. A grey-haired figure was busily engaged in digging in the garden at the front of the property.

Crabb assisted Lucy to alight from the trap.

'Good day to you,' said the man in the garden. 'You have come for the honey?'

'The honey?' asked Crabb.

'I keeps bees; they produce honey.'

'I see. No, we don't require any honey, thank you. Are you Mr Robinson? We believe that you were in charge of the Malvern police station some years ago.'

'That is so. How can I help you?' replied the man, laying aside his fork.

'I am Constable Crabb from the station in Ledbury, and this lady is Mrs Ravenscroft, the wife of Detective Inspector Ravenscroft.'

'Good day to you as well, Mrs Ravenscroft,' said the man, removing his cap. 'Ravenscroft, you say? I've heard good things about that fellow. He's solved quite a few crimes in the area, if I remember rightly.'

'That is so,' said Lucy, smiling.

'I've been retired for the past eight or nine years. I suspect you may be enquiring about one of my old cases.'

'Yes, sir. What do you recall about the death of Lizzie Warren?' asked Crabb.

'Lizzie Warren?' asked Robinson, giving Crabb a cautious look.

'About ten years ago. Lizzie Warren,' repeated the constable.

'Oh yes, that Lizzie Warren case. Poor girl; found dead on the hills. It was my last case, I remember, about a month before I retired.'

'How did she die, Mr Robinson?' asked Lucy.

'She'd fallen and hit the side of her head on one of the rocks. Been there for over a day when we found her. It was a sad way to go. I think she was only twenty or so,' muttered Robinson, shaking his head.

'There was no suggestion that someone could have killed her?' said Crabb.

'No. Whyever would you think so?'

'These things are possible, Mr Robinson,' replied the constable.

'Well we didn't suspect foul play. It was quite obvious to all of us that she'd been out walking over the hills by herself when she fell and had this terrible accident.'

'There was no sign of any other injuries?' asked Lucy.

'What other injuries, Mrs Ravenscroft?'

'That she might have been attacked in any way.'

'No, there was nothing of that nature,' answered Robinson, turning away and resuming his digging.

'We believe that the girl worked on a farm called The Orchards out at Parkway. Did you interview the farmer?' continued Crabb.

'Yes, Constable, but we didn't get very far.'

'Oh? Why is that, sir?'

'Farmer there, man called Rostagon, was surly and not very helpful. We did manage to find out that the girl had worked there on the farm for two or three years before her death, that was all.'

'Did you find out anything else?' persisted Crabb.

'What do you mean, anything else?'

'Did Mr Rostagon say what Lizzie was doing up in the hills when she had her accident?'

'I don't remember. I suppose he said she'd

gone for a walk or something like that,' said Robinson, thrusting his fork into the ground. 'It was all such a long time ago. I don't know why you want to drag all this up again. No amount of questions or enquiries now will bring poor Lizzie back, will it?'

'Was there a report?' asked Crabb.

'Of course there was a report, Constable. Look, I don't think there's anything else I can tell you about the case. It was just an unfortunate accident, and that's all there was to it. Now if you'll excuse me, I want to plant these seeds before the rains come,' said the former policeman, showing signs of irritation.

'Well, thank you, Mr Robinson. We won't detain you any longer,' said Crabb, realising that any more questions would only cause annoyance whilst probably adding nothing to what they knew already.

'Constable Crabb. Good day to you, Mrs Ravenscroft.'

'Good day to you, Mr Robinson,' said Lucy as she mounted the trap. 'Thank you for your assistance.'

The retired policeman resumed his digging as the trap made its way back onto the Wells road.

'Well he wasn't able to provide us with much information,' said Crabb.

'It was all such a long time ago.'

'I am sure I would have remembered all the details of such a major incident as that for many years afterwards.'

'Tom, do you think we might have time to go out to Parkway before it gets dark?' asked Lucy.

★ ★ ★

They continued their journey along the winding roads and over the railway line, the Malvern range always on their left, and past the Eastnor turn, until they eventually descended into the town of Ledbury. Here Crabb turned the horse sharply to the left onto the Gloucester road. A few minutes later they arrived at the small hamlet of Parkway.

'I think The Orchards is this way,' said Crabb, turning off to the left. The trap made its way up a well-worn rutted path that ran between fields of fruit trees and hops before eventually pulling up at the entrance to a large farm building. As they arrived, a barking sheepdog ran up towards them.

'Down, boy!' shouted a man emerging from inside a nearby stable. The dog snapped at Crabb before running over to its master. 'What do you want?' growled the man.

Lucy stepped down from the trap and observed the large heavily built man with untidy hair and of unshaven appearance, who was dressed in stained and muddy attire.

'We are the police,' announced Crabb. 'I presume you are Mr Rostagon?'

'I am, and who wants him?' came back the curt reply.

'We are from the police station in Ledbury. I am Constable Crabb and this lady is Mrs Ravenscroft, the wife of Detective Inspector Ravenscroft.'

'Since when have the police sent out their wives to make enquiries?' sneered the farmer, glaring at Lucy before turning his back on them both.

'We are making enquiries concerning Lizzie Warren,' said Crabb. 'We understand that she was in your employ.'

The farmer paused for a moment before speaking. 'I told the police at the time all about it. That's all I've got to say. Now I've got the milking to get on with.'

'We understand that she met with an accident on the hills,' said Lucy.

'Well if you knows that, what do you come bothering me for?' snapped Rostagon.

'Have a care, sir. Remember you are speaking to a lady,' interjected Crabb.

'That's as may be. I'm done with all this. Michael! Michael!' yelled the farmer, turning on his heel.

'Perhaps we should go, Mrs Ravenscroft,' whispered Crabb.

'Michael! Where the blazes is that lazy good-for-nothing when you want him? Ah, there you are. These are the police, wanting to know all about Lizzie. You remember Lizzie. You tell 'em; I'm busy,' mumbled a disinterested Rostagon, addressing a middle-aged man who had emerged from the house; then he and the dog disappeared into the barn.

'Lizzie?' asked the man, coming forward hesitantly.

'Yes, Lizzie Warren. We are making enquiries. I am Constable Crabb from the Ledbury police station, and this is Mrs Ravenscroft, the wife of the inspector,' said Crabb.

'But Lizzie, she been dead for over ten years,' stuttered the man, a strained expression on his face.

'Can I ask your name and occupation, sir?' enquired Crabb.

'Michael Sangster. I work for Mr Rostagon on the farm.'

'How long have you worked here?'

'Since I was a boy; nearly twenty years,' replied the man, giving Crabb and Lucy a vacant stare.

'So you knew Lizzie Warren quite well?'

'Aye, but she be dead.'

'I know. Can you tell us what happened on the day she died?'

'I don't remember,' said the man, suddenly turning away.

'It is very important, Michael, that we learn how Lizzie died,' said Lucy, seeking to calm the labourer's anxiety.

'I don't remember,' mumbled Sangster.

'Please help us,' reiterated Lucy.

'It were after lunch on a Sunday. Lizzie said she were going for a walk. That were the last I saw of her.'

'Did she say where she was going?' asked Crabb.

'No. She went off towards Eastnor.'

'Did you go after her?'

'No,' answered the man, showing a sudden look of fear.

'That's all right, Michael,' said Lucy. 'We mean you no harm. Can you tell us anything else about Lizzie?'

'Lizzie was nice,' recalled the man with a smile.

'She was kind to you?' asked Lucy.

'Aye. She were always doing things for us. She helped me with my reading and writing.'

'That was very good of her.'

'I can write my name.'

'I'm sure you can. Can you tell us if anyone

other than Mr Rostagon, you and Lizzie worked on the farm at the time of her accident?'

'No, there were just the three of us. Master's wife, she died fifteen year ago.'

'What kind of work did Lizzie do?'

'She milked the cows, worked in the dairy, did the cooking.'

'Did Lizzie have a young man courting her?' continued Lucy.

'What you want to know that for?'

'She must have been an attractive girl. She must have had admirers.'

'There was only him.'

'Who was that?'

'Don't know.'

'Come, man, you must know something,' said Crabb, finding that he was becoming irritated by the labourer's replies.

'Don't know.'

'How long had she known this man?' asked Lucy, trying to encourage the labourer to be more forthcoming with his replies.

'I don't know,' muttered Sangster, staring vacantly down at the ground.

'She must have spoken about this man,' said Crabb.

Sangster did not reply.

'I don't think we can obtain anything further from him, Mrs Ravenscroft.'

'Michael, was Lizzie going to meet that man on the day she went out to Eastnor?' asked Lucy.

'Don't know.'

'Are you sure about that?'

The labourer said nothing.

'Well thank you, Michael,' said Lucy before climbing back into the trap.

'If you can remember anything else, you can ask for me at the station in Ledbury,' instructed Crabb.

'Jacob,' mumbled the labourer.

'What was that you said?' asked Crabb.

'Jacob. She said he was Jacob.'

'Jacob!' exclaimed Lucy.

'Aye. She said she were going to meet Jacob.'

'Are you sure his name was Jacob?' asked Crabb.

'Aye, it were Jacob.'

'Thank you,' said Lucy.

'Drive on, boy,' said Crabb, urging the horse forward.

'Do you know what this means, Tom?' asked Lucy as the trap made its way down the lane.

'It means that Jacob did indeed come from around these parts, and that Lizzie Warren was going to meet him on the hills on that Sunday when she had the accident,' replied Crabb.

'This changes everything,' Lucy mused. 'I wonder whether Jacob could have played any part in Lizzie Warren's death.'

9

New York

Ravenscroft placed the knife and fork down on his plate.

'Food not to your liking then?' enquired the serving girl.

'I'm not particularly hungry,' the detective lied.

'Suit yourself, then; it's your loss,' said the girl, removing his plate. 'You want coffee?'

'Er . . . yes, please.'

After finding that he had unwittingly fallen asleep on his bed for most of the day, Ravenscroft had entered the dining room some sixty minutes earlier. The room was occupied by a dozen or so men, each of whom sat at a single table, in complete isolation from one another. He concluded that his fellow diners were all probably commercial travellers or clerks of a lower station in life. No one had communicated with any of the others during the meal, each having been busily engaged, between courses, in reading what Ravenscroft supposed was the local newspaper.

The greasy soup, of a green appearance, Ravenscroft had found both unappetizing and highly salty in taste; but at least it had been warm, and he had persisted with half of its contents before deciding to abandon the effort. This had been followed by a plate of overcooked vegetables, anaemic-looking mashed potatoes, and a piece of meat so tough in its texture that the detective would not have been surprised if someone had told him that it had originated from a labourer's leather boot.

'Coffee,' said the serving girl, interrupting his thoughts as she banged the tin mug down on the table before him, spilling some of the contents as she did so.

'Thank you. Tell me, have you worked here long?'

'Three weeks. What you want to know for?'

'No reason, really. It was just that a friend of mine . . . ' But before Ravenscroft could complete the sentence, the girl had turned away and was busily engaged in serving the man at the next table.

Ravenscroft took a sip of the coffee and found it surprisingly good. Turning towards the table that was nearest to him, he decided to break the silence of the room by addressing its occupant, a small, middle-aged, sour-looking man with a drooping moustache. 'Do you stay in this establishment very often?'

'Not if I can help it,' came back the curt reply.

Ravenscroft smiled. 'This is my first visit here.'

'Then I guess you won't be staying here again, buddy,' said the man without looking up from his paper.

'I guess not. May I ask why you stay here, then?' enquired Ravenscroft.

'It's cheap and convenient.'

'Have you been staying here long?'

'On and off — generally off — for the past five years. Why do you want to know?'

'It is just that a friend of mine was a resident here, but that was over ten years ago. I wondered whether you might remember him.'

'I've been coming here for fifteen years,' said a voice from the other side of the room.

'Then perhaps you might recall my friend? His name was Thomas Temple. He was also an Englishman like myself,' replied Ravenscroft.

'The name means nothing to me.'

'Never heard of him,' joined in another voice.

Ravenscroft drank his coffee and waited to see if anyone else in the room would be forthcoming, but he was met by a wall of silence and indifference.

'You want more coffee?' asked the girl, returning to the room.

'Yes, thank you.'

She replenished his mug before going on to the other tables. Ravenscroft drank the rest of his coffee and made his way out of the dining room, suddenly colliding with a man in the hallway. 'I'm most terribly sorry,' apologised the inspector.

'Think nothing of it,' said the tall dark-haired stranger, forcing a brief smile and raising his hat before turning the corner and quickly exiting the building.

'I wonder if I might have a word with Mrs Scrivens?' asked Ravenscroft, addressing the old man behind the reception desk.

'Leaving already? I knew you would. I said to Ma that you wouldn't last the day.'

'No, that is not my intention.'

'Us New Yorkers not good enough for you English, eh?'

'That is not the case. I would just like a few words with the proprietor, if you please.'

'What you want with Ma, then?'

'I would rather tell her, if you would be obliged,' said Ravenscroft, beginning to tire of the old man's abrasive manner.

'Ma! Ma!'

The door opened quickly. 'What you want? I'm busy,' growled the woman.

'Gent wants a word with you, Ma,' mumbled the man, moving to the far end of the counter.

'Room not good enough for you, I suppose?'

'The room is just fine.'

'Then I suppose it's the food,' said the woman, staring at Ravenscroft in a not entirely friendly way as her ample bosom leaned threateningly over the edge of the counter.

'No, it isn't the food.'

'What is it then?'

'I just require some information.'

'Information can be a dangerous thing in this town.'

'I believe a friend of mine, Thomas Temple, resided here. I just wondered whether you still remembered the gentleman at all?'

'Temple? You remember Temple?' the woman asked the clerk.

'I can't say as I do, Ma.'

'He was here about ten years ago,' continued Ravenscroft.

'No, can't remember him at all,' replied the woman firmly.

'He came over from England. He was the New York agent for a company called Mincing and Stricket.'

'What you want to know for?' asked Ma,

staring intently again at Ravenscroft.

'He was a friend of mine in England, then he came over to New York, and I haven't seen him since. I would rather like to make his acquaintance again, if at all possible,' said Ravenscroft, looking for the appropriate words and feeling increasingly uncomfortable.

'Temple!' laughed the old man.

'So you do remember him?'

'Oh yes, we remember him,' said Ma Scrivens, contradicting her earlier claim as she drew herself up to her full height and folded her arms in a defensive posture.

'Well, can you tell me where I might find him?'

'Hah, hah!' The old man continued laughing.

'Blackwell's, that's where you'll find him,' offered Ma.

'Blackwell's? Is that another lodging house?' asked Ravenscroft.

'Blackwell's a lodging house? Tell him, Ma,' laughed the old man.

'Blackwell's is a prison.'

'A prison!' exclaimed Ravenscroft. 'You mean Temple is in prison?'

'Yep — or rather he was. He got sent down for two or three years, I think,' said Ma, suddenly forthcoming with her answers.

'What was his crime?' asked a shocked Ravenscroft.

'Handling stolen goods; it was something to do with his work. I must say we were rather surprised. He always looked the type that would never hurt anybody. He was an English gent, not unlike you I suppose,' sniffed the landlady.

'I see. Can you tell me more about this prison, Blackwell's?'

'It's on one of the islands.'

'How would I get there?'

'Take the ferry from East 26th Street.'

'Thank you. Was that the last you heard of him?' enquired Ravenscroft, anxious to capitalize on his questioning now that the couple were less guarded with their answers.

'Haven't seen him from the day he got sent down,' Ma said.

'I don't suppose you know where the offices of Mincing and Stricket are?'

'Down by the docks. Write it down for you if you like,' offered Ma, adopting a more helpful tone.

'That would be most kind of you. I shall call upon them shortly.'

'That all?' enquired the old man, stroking his beard.

'Yes, thank you. I'm most obliged for your assistance,' said Ravenscroft, accepting the scrap of paper from the landlady.

'I wouldn't go there this evening. It's getting dark now. It's not safe around that area down by the docks,' said Ma.

'Thank you for your advice.'

Ravenscroft made his way back to his room, up the three flights of stairs. He had been startled by the news that Temple had been sent to prison. That would explain why he had broken off all contact with Mincing and Stricket in London. The landlady had told him that Temple had been sentenced for handling stolen goods, and that the term of his incarceration had been two or three years. Now that he knew where and how to reach the penitentiary, he resolved that the next morning he would take the ferry across to the institution and see if the authorities there could provide him with any more information regarding Maria Constantine's son.

But he also had the address of where the young man had worked before his imprisonment. Had Temple stolen goods from his employers? If so, why had not Mincing and Stricket mentioned this fact to Lucy when she had visited them in London? They had merely said that all contact with Temple had been lost. He wondered whether Mincing and Stricket had forgotten the real reason for not hearing from their employee, or whether they had been unwilling to disclose the truth. At least he now had the address of the warehouse. Perhaps people there would be more forthcoming about the fate of the former apprentice from the Foundling Hospital. He also wondered whether Temple might have changed his name to Jacob upon his release from the prison, in order to hide his guilty past — but then he reminded himself that perhaps Temple and Jacob had been two different men rather than the same person.

As Ravenscroft lay down on his bed, he felt reassured that although he had not found Temple still living in Scrivens' Boarding House, he had at least two new avenues to explore in the morning, and perhaps one of those places might lead him eventually to Temple himself.

⋆   ⋆   ⋆

Ravenscroft alighted from the cab at the quayside, and following the directions the cabman had given him, made his way down the cobbled street. On either side of him men were busy loading carts and wagons with parcels of goods from the warehouses, whilst others were securing large wooden crates to platforms that were being pulled up to openings situated on the upper floors of the buildings.

Reaching the end of the quay, Ravenscroft turned to his right and found that he was walking along a narrower, darker and quieter alleyway that ran alongside the water. After a few hundred yards an old warehouse came into view, and as he drew nearer he was rewarded by the words 'Mincing and Stricket' appearing in faded letters on the side of the building.

He made his way up a flight of old wooden steps that had clearly seen better days, as each one creaked loudly with the sound of his feet, whereas others were in such a state of disrepair that he could see the ground below him in several places where the wood had decayed. Eventually reaching a small landing at the top of the flight, he was disappointed to find that the door was tightly secured with a large padlock. As he looked up at the grimy windows and surveyed the state of the neglected building, he wondered whether the premises had been left vacant for many years. Frustrated that he had come this far only for this line of enquiry to come to nothing, Ravenscroft now retraced his way carefully down the rotting staircase.

Deciding that the New York operation of Mincing and Stricket had ceased with Temple's conviction, Ravenscroft decided to see if there was perhaps another entrance to the building located round the corner, but again he found only a brick wall. The noise of a cab drawing up outside the main entrance startled him, and he instinctively peered round the corner to see who the new arrival was.

'You need not wait,' said a familiar voice.

As the man walked across to the steps, Ravenscroft recognised him as Petters from his time on the *Etruria*. The detective drew further back round the building so that he could observe the new arrival without giving away his own presence. He watched as the man walked up the steps and took out a key from his pocket to open the padlock on the door, before entering the warehouse.

Ravenscroft's first instinct had been to climb the steps, to enter and declare himself to Petters, but then he remembered the warning he had been given on the ship, and decided to remain hidden. He knew that Petters was one of O'Callaghan's associates. Now it seemed as though these men had some connection with Mincing and Stricket. Had they also known Temple? And if so, had the poor unfortunate Englishman been implicated in some unlawful activity in which they had all been complicit? Had Temple changed his name to Jacob after his time in prison, and eventually made his way back to

England? O'Callaghan and his associates had returned to New York on the *Etruria*, so they must have been in England before. Could they have tracked down Jacob and strung up his body on Hangman Hill, perhaps because he had betrayed them all those years ago? These thoughts seemed to tumble into the inspector's mind in quick succession; and the more he reflected on the matter, the more unanswered questions seemed to present themselves.

After a few minutes had elapsed, the noise of footsteps on the creaking boards alerted him to the fact that Petters was now leaving the warehouse. He peered round the corner and saw that the man was carrying what appeared to be a brown paper parcel. Ravenscroft watched as the man walked back up the narrow alleyway and out of sight, then waited for two or three minutes before venturing forth. A quick glance up to the landing showed him that Petters had again secured the padlock.

He wondered what was inside the old warehouse. Although the building did not look as though it had been used for years, it nevertheless must contain some items of worth, as Petters had collected a parcel from inside. The inspector's curiosity had been aroused, and he knew that he would need to gain access to the interior of the building and make a search of the premises. He decided that he would return later, when darkness had fallen, and see what secrets the warehouse held.

* * *

Ravenscroft boarded the ferry and looked out across the harbour as the vessel began to make the short crossing to Blackwell's Island.

'You visiting someone there?' enquired one of the old seamen.

'Yes,' replied Ravenscroft.

'Better than staying there, I'd be bound.'

'Yes, I would not wish to do that.'

'Do you see those buildings over there? They house nearly two thousand prisoners.'

'That is rather a lot.'

'And that building to the side is the workhouse.'

'So the poor and infirm live there as well as the criminal classes?'

'Sure do.'

'What is that building at the end of the island?'

'Oh, that's the old lighthouse.'

'How long is the island?'

'It's about two miles in length. It must be hard for the poor devils inside to look out of their cell windows and see the waters and the houses on the other side of the harbour, and realise what they've lost.'

'Indeed. Have any of the prisoners ever escaped?'

'They do from time to time, but they don't get very far. If the sea doesn't get 'em, the law usually catches up with 'em before long. You're not from around these parts, then?'

'No. I have come from England.'

'England. That's a long way to have come.'

'It is indeed.'

'Ferry will be there in a few minutes. The return trip is on the hour, every hour, till dusk.'

'Thank you. You have been most informative.'

A few minutes later, Ravenscroft alighted from the ferry. He looked up at the austere uniform buildings ahead and decided to make his way up the cobbled pathway towards the central block. As he passed a group of men dressed in prison uniforms who were busily engaged in laying bricks for the foundations of a new building, one of the wardens raised his cap in acknowledgement.

'Good morning,' said Ravenscroft. 'Can you tell me if I am going in the right direction to the main office?'

'Indeed, sir. Just follow the path to the front door over there,' replied the warden, pointing.

'Thank you.'

Upon reaching the front entrance, Ravenscroft pushed open the door and found that he had entered a large hallway.

'Can I help you, sir?' asked a clerk, coming forward to meet him.

'Good morning. My name is Detective Inspector Ravenscroft from England. I would like to speak with the warden if I may. Perhaps you'd be good enough to give him my card.'

'You've come rather a long way,' sniffed the clerk, accepting the card. 'If you'd care to take a seat over there, sir, I'll ask whether the warden will see you.'

'Thank you.'

Ravenscroft watched as the clerk made his way up a winding staircase, before seating himself on one of the straight-backed chairs. As he looked around the hall, he observed a number of paintings on the walls and deduced that each of them was probably a portrait of one of the previous wardens.

After a few minutes he was rewarded by the sight of a grey-haired elderly gentleman making his way down the stairs, the clerk following on behind him. 'Good morning. Your card says that you're Detective Inspector Ravenscroft from England.'

'That is indeed so.'

'It isn't every day that we have a visit from a policeman from England. I hope you're not checking up on all us errant Yanks? We did obtain our independence over a hundred years ago,' laughed the warden.

'Indeed you did, sir; and from what I've seen of New York so far, you seem to be making a good job of it.'

'It's kind of you to say so, Mr Ravenscroft. Now how can I be of assistance to you?'

'I would like some information regarding one of your previous inmates.'

'One of our past inmates, you say? Then I think you'd better come into the office where we keep all our records.'

Ravenscroft followed the warden into a large room that led off the hall.

'What name are you looking for?' said the warden, sitting down in a large leather armchair.

'The name of the prisoner was Thomas Temple. I believe he was sentenced to two or three years' imprisonment here, approximately ten years ago,' said Ravenscroft, accepting the seat that had been indicated.

'Finch, if you'll be so good,' instructed the warden, addressing the clerk.

'Yes, sir,' said the young man, busily opening a number of cabinets at the side of the room.

'May I ask what your interest is in this man?' asked the warden, leaning back in his chair and arching his fingers beneath his chin as he stared at Ravenscroft.

'A few weeks ago we found the body of a man on one of the hills near the town where I live,' began an apprehensive Ravenscroft. 'He'd been hung up from one of the trees. At first we were unable to identify him, but our enquiries eventually lead us to your city. It was the landlady of the house where Temple resided who told me of his crime and punishment.'

'Forgive me, Mr Ravenscroft, but why have you come all this way to find out about a man who's dead? I'd have thought that your detective skills would have been put to better use in your own country.'

'I know this may seem strange, but we're not certain that the dead man was indeed called Thomas Temple. I have to find out what happened to the man when he came to America so I can ascertain whether he was the victim, or someone who was involved in his murder; hence the reason for visiting you today.'

'I see. The name means nothing to me, but I only came to the island three years ago, and young Finch here has only been with us for less than a year.'

'Fifteen months, sir,' interjected the young man, placing a folder on the desk.

'Fifteen months. I stand corrected, Finch. Now let's see what we have here. "Thomas Temple. Born England; sentenced to two years and three months imprisonment for dealing in stolen goods. Prisoner showed good conduct; released on time." I'm afraid that is all it says.'

'There is no photograph?'

'No. We do sometimes take photographs of our prisoners, but there doesn't appear to be one here.'

'I wonder whether it would be possible to discover what happened to Temple when he left the prison?' asked a somewhat disappointed Ravenscroft.

'Well yes, I think we might be able to assist you there. There's a note made in pencil to say that Temple secured employment at Macy and Co.'

'What is that?'

'Macy's is a New York department store.'

'I see. Forgive me, but is it usual practice for the penitentiary to secure employment for its prisoners upon their release?'

'Not usually, but as the note was made by my predecessor, I can only conclude that this was some kind of special case. Perhaps the warden felt that your man Temple was

194

deserving of a new start in life, and somehow used his influence in securing the position for him.'

'That is most interesting. Is there anything else in the prisoner's file that may be of relevance?'

'No; it would appear as though Temple was a model prisoner. Macy's is an important department store here in New York. It wouldn't have taken on Temple lightly. I have no doubt that the warden's personal recommendation helped in this case.'

'So it would appear. Thank you both for your assistance,' said Ravenscroft, rising from his seat.

'I'm glad we've been able to help you, Mr Ravenscroft. What will you do now?'

'Follow the trail to Macy's. I would be obliged if you could tell me where I might find the store.'

'Of course. Macy and Co. is along 18th Street.'

'Thank you.'

★ ★ ★

Later that afternoon, Ravenscroft looked up at the sign above the doorway of a large building which bore the letters 'R.H. Macy and Co'. Entering the store, he found himself in what appeared to be a large room with counters running along the walls and down the centre.

'Can I help you, sir?' said a doorman.

'Yes; I require some information concerning your store. I wonder whether I could speak with someone who may be able to assist me in my quest?'

'Certainly, sir. Come with me.'

'Thank you,' said Ravenscroft, following the man as he walked down the aisle of busy shoppers towards a central staircase.

'Gentleman would like to speak with someone in authority,' said the doorman, addressing a tall, thin lady standing by one of the counters.

'And what is the nature of your enquiry, sir?' asked the lady.

'I am an English policeman. I require some information regarding one of your employees. Perhaps I could have a word with the manager of the store?'

'Certainly, sir. If you'll follow me.'

Ravenscroft followed the assistant up a flight of stairs.

'Gentleman to see the manager,' said the assistant, addressing a young woman at the top of the staircase.

'Oh my, do please follow me sir,' said the woman, smiling.

Ravenscroft followed her up the next flight of steps. 'I guess you're not from around these parts?' she asked.

'Your assumption is correct. I have come from England.'

'England! My, how quaint is that!' she giggled.

Ravenscroft smiled.

'English gentleman to see Mr Gordon,' said the woman, speaking to a more elderly and serious woman at the top of the stairs.

'Good morning,' said Ravenscroft.

'He's from England,' giggled the first woman, giving Ravenscroft a broad smile before skipping down the stairs.

'Please follow me, sir,' said the more serious shop assistant.

As Ravenscroft followed this new attendant through the aisle of counters and up another two flights of stairs, he was beginning to wonder whether he would ever arrive at his destination.

'English gentleman to see Mr Gordon,' said the woman, addressing a young clerk.

'Would you care to follow me, sir?' said the young man.

Ravenscroft thanked the female assistant and followed the young man up a further two flights of stairs, then along a brightly painted corridor until they reached a closed door.

'I'll see if someone can assist you, sir,' said the man, knocking on the door.

'Yes, Murray?' asked an elderly man, opening the door.

'Gentleman would like a word with Mr Gordon, sir.'

'Well I'm afraid that won't be possible. Mr Gordon is very busy at present. He can't possibly see anyone today. You shouldn't have brought the gentleman up here.'

'Forgive me, sir,' said Ravenscroft, stepping forward and taking out his card from his coat pocket. 'My name is Detective Inspector Ravenscroft. I have come all the way from England on a most urgent matter.'

'You should have written first; could have saved you the journey,' replied the man in what Ravenscroft considered a lofty manner.

'It is most imperative that I have a word with the manager. It concerns one of your employees,' persisted the detective.

The man studied the card.

'I will not take up more than a few minutes of your manager's time.'

'Wait here,' replied the man abruptly, closing the door in Ravenscroft's face.

The young man looked upwards, then smiled and shuffled his feet, as Ravenscroft felt himself becoming more and more frustrated.

'He's a busy man,' remarked the young man after a full minute had elapsed.

'I see,' sighed Ravenscroft.

'Sorry, but Mr Gordon is far too busy today,' said the elderly clerk, opening the door once more. 'You'll have to make an appointment. Perhaps he'll see you next week.'

'I don't have the time to make an appointment. Will you kindly inform Mr Gordon that this is a very important criminal matter, and that it is imperative that I see him without delay,' said a tense Ravenscroft, raising his voice.

'No need for annoyance, sir,' reprimanded the man.

'Then please tell your Mr Gordon that I must see him now.'

'What's all that noise, Fothergill?' boomed out a voice from within.

Ravenscroft, deciding that it was time now to seize the opportunity, quickly brushed past the elderly clerk and strode into the office.

'You can't go in there,' protested the man.

'What the blazes is going on?' said a fat red-faced man seated behind a large desk at the rear of the room.

'Forgive the intrusion, sir, but I must have words with you on a most urgent matter,' began Ravenscroft.

'I'm sorry, Mr Gordon — I did tell the gentleman that you were otherwise engaged,' stuttered Fothergill.

'Oh, it's of no matter. 'Detective', it says here,' said Gordon, looking at Ravenscroft's card. 'You're from England as well. Hell, you sure have come a long way, mister.'

'I have indeed.'

'Well I suppose I can give you two minutes. Time is money, you know.'

'Yes.'

'Well, get on with it then.'

'I am investigating a murder that took place a few weeks ago in England. We have reason to believe that one of your employees was implicated. His name is Thomas Temple,' said Ravenscroft, anxious to condense his request into as few words as possible.

'Name means nothing to me. Temple, you say? Look out his file, Fothergill.'

'Yes, sir.'

Gordon resumed his writing as the clerk searched through a large cabinet in the corner of the room, muttering aloud as he did so.

'You have a most impressive store here,' said Ravenscroft, attempting to break the silence.

'Macy's is the best in New York,' Gordon replied.

'I expect so.'

'I say so,' emphasised Gordon. 'Soon all the cities in the world will be full of these stores. You have any in your town in England?'

'No, we only have small shops.'

'Well you mark my words, it won't be long before there is one.'

'I very much doubt that,' said Ravenscroft with a smile.

'Your London should take a leaf out of our book and build department stores. The day of the small shop is over, I promise you that,' said Gordon, lighting up a large cigar.

'The file, sir,' said Fothergill, placing a folder on his superior's desk.

'Now let's see what we have here,' said Gordon, opening the file and beginning to read. 'Thomas Temple — Born England; period of employment June 1884 until August 1885. Employed in china department.' That's all. No, wait a moment. 'Reason for termination of employment — employee wished to return to home country.'

'He returned to England!' exclaimed Ravenscroft.

'That's what it says here, in black and white.'

'It doesn't say how he obtained employment in your store?'

'No.'

'You don't have a photograph of Mr

Temple, by any chance?' asked a disappointed Ravenscroft.

'No.'

'And there is nothing else in the file about his conduct or his appearance?'

'No. The rest of the file is empty.'

'He must have been quite an impressive young man,' interjected Fothergill.

'Oh? Why do you say that?' asked Ravenscroft.

'China is our most lucrative department. Nearly a third of all our sales come from there. We tend to place the most presentable of our staff in that section.'

'I see.'

'Well if that is all, Mr . . . er?' said Gordon.

'Ravenscroft.'

'Mr Ravenscroft. You must excuse me. Time is important to us all here at Macy's.' With that, he resumed his writing.

Fothergill coughed; and Ravenscroft, realising that nothing more could be gained by prolonging the interview, rose from his chair.

'Enjoy your time in New York, Mr Ravenscroft. Hope you catch who you're after,' said Gordon without looking up from his papers.

'Thank you,' answered Ravenscroft as he made his way towards the door.

'Why not buy the little lady at home

something pretty on your way out of the store,' shouted Gordon as Ravenscroft closed the door behind him.

★ ★ ★

Later that evening, Ravenscroft paid off the cabman and began to walk down the cobbled street at the side of the docks, his thoughts turning to what he had discovered earlier that day. The trail had led him from Ma Scrivens' Lodging House, to the penitentiary on Blackwell's Island where he had learned of Temple's criminal record, and then on to Macy's Department Store, and all the time he had thought that he was getting nearer to his quarry. But then had come the final blow that Thomas Temple had left New York and returned to England some six or seven years previously. He had come all this way in the hope of finding Temple, only now to discover that the man was no longer resident in the city. It seemed as though the trail had come to an abrupt end. There would be nothing else for it but to return home and tell Maria Constantine that he no longer knew the whereabouts of her son.

Ravenscroft had no proof that Temple had indeed returned to England. The fact that he had seen Petters collecting a parcel from the former warehouse of Mincing and Stricket earlier that day, and that he had learnt that Temple had worked for that company before being sent to prison for 'receiving stolen goods', strongly suggested that Temple had been an associate of O'Callaghan's. Could Temple have lied when he had left Macy's? Perhaps he had not returned to England at all, but had resumed his criminal activities with this New York gang.

The more he thought about the case, the more the inspector became convinced that he had to know what was inside that warehouse. The answers to all his questions could be found there. There might be records inside that would tell him more about Temple's whereabouts; and if he could find evidence of O'Callaghan's criminal activities, he could then go to the police authorities in New York.

Then he had considered how best to gain access to the warehouse. To break into the building in daylight risked being suddenly discovered by anyone who happened to be walking past the premises. Likewise, if he were to enter when it was dark, he would need a lantern to light his way, and he then risked that the bright light would draw attention to himself. Finally he had decided to return to the warehouse as the afternoon light was fading, when the area would probably be quieter, and yet there would be enough light to enable him to find his way into the building.

Reaching the bottom of the steps, Ravenscroft looked hastily behind him; and, being satisfied that there was no one present, he climbed the old creaking stairs and forced the padlock from its fixture. Finding the door still locked, he placed his shoulder against the rotting woodwork and was rewarded by the ease with which the door gave way.

He stood for some minutes in what at first sight appeared to be an empty room, but after a few seconds his eyes adjusted to the gloomy interior and he observed a desk and some shelves at the far end. On the desk lay a large number of papers. Ravenscroft thumbed through the pile, straining to see the writing on some of the pages, but he could not make sense of any of the contents.

He turned his attention to the shelves located to either side of the desk. Here several wooden packing cases were stacked. He moved several of the cases, but could find no writing on the outside which might have suggested what lay inside. Taking one of the wooden boxes over towards the desk, he prised open the top. He peered into the case, and after pulling the straw to one side he placed his hand inside, drew it out, and discovered that he was clutching a collection of necklaces, rings and other fine jewellery.

'I think you should put that back inside the box, Mr Ravenscroft!'

The inspector turned round quickly and found that he was staring into the bright light of a lantern. Shielding his eyes from the glare, he made out the figure of Petters holding a gun in his direction.

'Dear, dear me, Mr Ravenscroft, what do we have here?'

Ravenscroft recognised the voice of O'Callaghan; and as the American came into view he also noticed Foy and one or two other men who were unknown to him.

'We thought you might return. Mr Petters here noticed you looking around outside earlier today. You should have been more careful. Curiosity is a dangerous thing, Mr Ravenscroft. Tie him to the chair, Foy,' instructed O'Callaghan.

Ravenscroft found that he was being seized by two of the men and being rudely thrust into the chair as Foy wrapped a rope tightly round his legs and arms.

'Well, Mr Ravenscroft, just who are you?' demanded O'Callaghan after taking a pull on a large cigar. 'We don't believe all that nonsense about butterflies.'

'It's the truth; I am a butterfly collector,'

protested Ravenscroft, knowing that the men were unlikely to believe him. 'I don't know what all this is about.'

'I'll make him talk,' growled Foy, drawing out a nasty-looking metal object from his pocket. 'He'll be in the pay of them damn Pinkertons.'

'I tell you I am nothing to do with any of the authorities. I have come to your country for peaceful purposes,' Ravenscroft persisted, feeling the sweat breaking out on his brow.

'Let me do him over,' threatened Foy, edging closer. 'I'll enjoy cutting him into little pieces.'

'Wait!' shouted O'Callaghan. 'I want to know what he's been up to. There could be more of them. You might as well tell us the truth, Mr Ravenscroft. Mr Foy here can be very persuasive, I assure you, and it will save you a lot of pain.'

'All right. I'm an English detective,' admitted Ravenscroft.

'I knew it!' said Foy. 'Let me finish him off now!'

'The authorities know I'm here.'

'Don't make me laugh,' said O'Callaghan, blowing smoke into Ravenscroft's face. 'No one knows you're here. After we're finished with you, you'll be thrown into the harbour, where you'll sink to the bottom of the sea and be eaten by the fishes. Your people at home will never know how you died.'

'Is that what you did to Temple all those years ago?'

'Temple? What's he talking about?' growled Petters.

'I've only come over here to find out what happened to Temple. I'm not interested in your activities,' pleaded Ravenscroft.

'Too late for that now, Mr Ravenscroft!' snapped O'Callaghan. 'You shouldn't have wandered in here tonight. That was such a foolish thing to do. We can't possibly let you go now. You know too much about our operation.'

'Look, I'm sure we can come to some arrangement,' said a frightened Ravenscroft, realising that he was pleading for his life.

'Arrangement!' O'Callaghan sneered. 'You English, always the same, so damned polite. We don't need to come to any 'arrangement'. You're a stupid man, Ravenscroft, and your stupidity will now be the death of you. You should've kept out of our affairs. I'm bored by all this. Shoot him, Foy, and then throw him into the river!'

'Please, don't do this,' begged Ravenscroft, thinking of Lucy and his children.

'Foy!' commanded O'Callaghan.

Ravenscroft closed his eyes.

A shot rang out!

10

Herefordshire

'Ravenscroft here?'

Crabb looked up from behind the desk in Ledbury police station.

'Are you deaf, man? I asked if Ravenscroft was here,' said the tall, heavily moustached and broad-whiskered man before Crabb could answer.

'I'm afraid the inspector is away at present, sir.'

'When will he be back?'

'I'm afraid I'm unable to say at the present time.'

'Unable to say? What kind of answer is that?' growled the new arrival.

'I'm sorry, sir, but it's the only answer I can give at the moment. The inspector is out of the country, and we don't know when he will return.'

'Well that's damn inconvenient. Damn inconvenient. Who are you, then?'

'I am Constable Crabb. I'm in charge during the inspector's absence,' he said with a smile, hoping to placate the aggressive man, but realising that he would probably not succeed.

'Damn it! I suppose you'll have to do then,'

replied the man grudgingly.

'How can I help you, sir?'

'I wish to report a burglary.'

'May I take down some details?' said Crabb, reaching for his pencil.

'Colonel Wendover. Army. Retired.'

'I assume that it's your house that has been burgled, Colonel?'

'You assume correct, Constable.'

'When did this burglary take place?'

'Don't rightly know.'

'You don't rightly know?'

'Don't repeat everything that I say, man!'

'I'm sorry, sir. Could I have your address?'

'Ashanti, Much Marcle.'

'That's a rather unusual name for a house, if I may say so,' remarked Crabb, writing down the details.

'Ashanti. I fought the blighters in '73.'

'I see. You say that you're not certain when the burglary took place?'

'My wife and I have been away for the past four weeks; been taking the air and all that in Eastbourne. House has been closed up. It was only when we returned yesterday that we discovered the burglary had taken place during our absence.'

'I see. Was there much damage?'

'The safe was broken into. The damn blighters took my wife's jewellery, my medals and fifty pounds that were all inside. I tell you that if I get hold of them, they won't be able to sit down for a year!'

'Was anything else taken from the house?'

'No, they seemed to have left everything else. Good job they didn't get the Ming vases. Went straight for the safe, they did.'

'Would you be able to provide me with a list of items that were taken?'

'Wrote them down here,' said Wendover, producing a piece of paper from his pocket and slapping it down on the counter.

'Thank you,' said Crabb, picking up the list and studying its contents.

'Now what I want to know is, what are you going to do about it?'

'You say the house was shut up during your stay in Eastbourne. May I ask if you have any servants?'

'Yes. Roberts — he's my man — he came with us. I sent the housekeeper and maid away for the month.'

'Have they been with you long?'

'Yes. Ah, see what you're getting at; inside job and all that. Sorry to disappoint you, Constable. Roberts has been with me for over twenty years. He was my batman during my army days. He is entirely loyal. Mrs Glencoe, the housekeeper, has been with us since we moved here fifteen years ago, and Mary the maid for five years. If any of them wanted to rob me, they would have done it long ago. Barking up the wrong tree there, I'm afraid.'

'Did anyone of a strange appearance call at the house before you left for Eastbourne?' asked Crabb, trying to think of all the questions he could.

'No; can't recall anyone.'

'I see.'

'What do you mean, 'I see'? Stop saying that, man; it's damned annoying. I want to know what you're going to do about it. My wife was very attached to her jewels, and my medals can't be replaced. Damn the devils!'

'I will come over this afternoon and inspect the damage.'

'Huh, a fat lot of good that will do. Whoever broke into my safe knew what they were up to.'

'I agree, sir, but it will help our enquiries if I could see the scene of the crime,' said Crabb, laying down his pencil on the counter.

'I suppose it will do no harm,' said Wendover, pulling a sour face.

'I will also circulate your list of stolen items to other police stations in the area, and make enquiries at jewellers in Ledbury, Hereford and Worcester.'

'You think the scoundrels will try and sell them?'

'It is possible, sir. Thieves will often try to either sell or pawn items they have stolen.'

'Right, Constable, we'll see you sharpish this afternoon. We want our possessions found.'

'We will endeavour to do our best for you.' Wendover nodded and strode briskly out of the office.

★ ★ ★

Later that afternoon, Crabb closed the door of 'Ashanti' in the Herefordshire village of Much Marcle, having just viewed the scene of the robbery, and fresh from his attempts to reassure both Colonel Wendover and his distressed wife that he would do all he could to recover their lost property. Now he decided to walk into the village, and as he drew near to the medieval church he saw an old man cutting the grass at the edge of the road.

'Good day to you,' said Crabb, addressing the man.

'Good day to ye, Constable,' replied the old man, pausing from his labours and wiping his brow. 'Dear me, 'tis hard work, this cutting. I be all of a swither. You have been to the colonel's, no doubt.'

'I have indeed.'

'It were a bad thing, that burglary. The

213

colonel didn't deserve that. It's a sad state of affairs if a man and his wife can't go away from their home without it being burgled like that.'

'News travels fast.'

'There's nothing that goes on in Much Marcle that I don't know about,' said the man with a grin.

'Can you tell me whether you have seen any strangers in the area during the past month or so?' asked Crabb.

'No, I don't think so. There was only that man who put that poster yonder some weeks ago,' replied the man, pointing to a tree outside the church.

'What poster?'

'Why, that poster that were advertising the fair in Ledbury. I don't hold with fairs much. Waste of both money and time, if you asks me.'

'I wonder if you could describe this man for me?' asked Crabb, taking out his notebook.

'Two of them, there were. There was the tall man; bit of a noddy he were. He had a long white beard. I remember he had a brightly coloured yellow waistcoat. Bit of a show-off if you ask me, wearing a waistcoat like that. 'E's a faddy and no mistake,' replied the man, warming to his subject.

'Can you tell me what the other man looked like?'

'He were younger than the other one, that's all I can say about him. Tell you the truth, I didn't take too much notice of them. They weren't here long. They were in a bit of a hespil, if you ask me.'

'Hespil?' asked Crabb, looking up from his notebook.

'Aye, hespil, you know? They were in a hurry.'

'I see. Well thank you for your information, my man.'

'Glad to have been of assistance. We must all help the law.'

Crabb returned to the trap deep in thought. After a moment's deliberation, he urged the horse forward.

* * *

'Good day to you, Constable Crabb,' said the elderly, uniformed, cheery-faced police officer.

'Good day to you, Sergeant Morris,' said Crabb.

'And what brings you to Hereford? Inspector Ravenscroft is not with you, then?'

'No, the inspector is away in America.'

'America? What's his nibs doing there?'

'He's following up a possible line of enquiry.'

'It seems a long way to go on an enquiry.

Wish they'd send me to America on police business. Still, some folk have all the luck. So Ravenscroft has left you in charge, me lad, has he?'

'Yes, Sergeant.'

'And what can we do for you?'

'I have just visited Much Marcle. Gentleman by the name of Wendover has had his house broken into and several items taken whilst he was away. I wondered whether you've had any similar burglaries in your area.'

'Let me see,' said the sergeant, consulting a large ledger on his desk. 'Ah yes, big house just outside Hereford was burgled some weeks ago. Some items of jewellery were taken.'

'When was this?'

'Sometime in early October, I think.'

'I knew it!' exclaimed Crabb. 'Tell me, Sergeant, do you recall if the travelling fair was here at that same time?'

'Let's have a look. Ah yes, it was the same week. I see that several arrests were made for drunkenness and disorderly conduct at the fair. Why, lad? What are you getting at?' asked Morris, looking up at Crabb.

'The Much Marcle burglary probably took place when the fair was in Ledbury. An old man there recollects seeing two men from the

216

fair putting up posters in the village.'

'And you think these men from the fair were on the lookout for properties that were unattended?'

'Yes.'

'You could well be onto something here, Constable Crabb.'

'After the fair left Ledbury, it went onto Tewkesbury.'

'Wait here, lad,' said Morris, disappearing into the next room before returning a few seconds later holding a collection of papers. 'Tewkesbury, you say? I remember reading about something . . . Yes, here we are. A report of a burglary at a house along the Gloucester road just outside the town.'

'When did that take place, Sergeant Morris?' asked Crabb, consulting his note-book.

'About a week after the fair left here.'

'And after it had been to Ledbury,' said an increasingly animated Crabb. 'After Tewkes-bury, I believe the fair went on to Evesham.'

'Yes; here we are, Crabb. Similar breaking and entering just outside Evesham a few days later.'

'I knew it! Shortly before the fair arrives in a town, Rockstone and his accomplice go round the nearby areas, putting up posters and looking out for empty properties that they can enter after it's dark and everyone has gone to the fair.'

'Sorry, but who is this Rockstone?' asked a perplexed Morris.

'He's the man we've been seeking in connection with the hanging on the Malvern Hills. He's a showman, selling quack medicines at the fair.'

'I remember reading about the murder in the local newspaper. Nobody seemed to know the name of the dead man. Where is this Rockstone now?'

'I'm afraid we don't know. We've been searching everywhere for him.'

'Well I must congratulate you, Constable Crabb, on an excellent piece of criminal deduction.'

'Thank you, Sergeant.'

'What we need to do now is find out where that fair of yours is at the present time. The fact that these burglaries have continued after the fair left Ledbury suggests to me that this Rockstone has returned to his companions.'

'I think you are correct, Sergeant.'

'Find the whereabouts of this fair, keep them under observation, and catch them in the act. We will have them, lad!' said Morris, rubbing his hands enthusiastically. 'We will have this Rockstone fellow. Yes we will. I say again, well done to you, Constable Crabb.'

★   ★   ★

'Good morning, Mr Clifford,' said Lucy, entering the Malvern Reading Rooms.

'Good morning to you, Mrs Ravenscroft,' replied the librarian, giving a little bow. 'May I say how pleasant it is to see you again.'

'Thank you, Mr Clifford.'

'I trust your husband is well?'

'Very well, thank you, as far as I know.'

'I believe that you may be after further information.'

'Indeed. You may recall that when Constable Crabb and I visited you last week, you were able to show us the newspaper report concerning the death of Lizzie Warren.'

'Yes. You would like to see the report again?'

'If I may. I would be most obliged.'

'Please follow me, my good lady.'

Lucy followed the librarian into the back room.

'If you'd care to take a seat, I will bring over the volume for you,' said Clifford with a smile.

'Thank you,' said Lucy, removing her gloves before sitting at the table.

'I think this was the volume,' said Clifford after a few moments had elapsed. 'If you'll excuse me, I will have to leave you to your

219

own devices, as I believe another customer may have just entered the library.'

'Thank you, Mr Clifford. You've been most helpful.'

Lucy opened the large volume as the librarian departed the room, and began to turn over the pages until she found the report of Lizzie Warren's death. As she read again the words describing the tragedy on the hills, she recalled the visit that she and Tom Crabb had made to the farm at Parkway, where the unfortunate girl had worked, and from where she had last been seen by Michael Sangster on that fateful morning walking out towards the hills.

Then she turned over the pages where she again found the report of the inquest — 'Death Caused by Misadventure'. Had Lizzie Warren died as the result of a fall on Hangman Hill, or had Jacob been involved in her death? Sangster had said that Lizzie was being courted by Jacob. Had the lovers met up on the hill? If so, had they quarrelled with the result that Jacob had killed Lizzie? If that had been the case, it would also explain why Jacob had been unwilling to return to the area where the tragedy had taken place.

After some moments of thought, Lucy decided to turn over more of the pages of the newspaper, but could find no further mention of the case in that week's issue. Turning to the next weekly issue, she was suddenly surprised to find the entry she had been seeking:

FUNERAL OF LIZZIE WARREN.
The funeral took place last Thursday morning, at Little Malvern Priory, of Lizzie Warren, who met with a tragic accident on Hangman Hill. We understand that no relatives were present at the service and burial, as it appears that Miss Warren was quite alone in this world. Mourners included her employer, Mr S. Rostagon of The Orchards, Parkway, and Mr Michael Sangster, a fellow employee. Also present were Mr Francis Constantine of The Verzons, Trumpet, near Ledbury, and . . .

Lucy read again the words 'Also present were Mr Francis Constantine of The Verzons' and sat back in her chair in dismay. Why had Francis Constantine attended Lizzie Warren's funeral? The Orchards and The Verzons were several miles apart, so he could not have gone out of respect as a near neighbour. What, then, had been the connection between the Herefordshire landowner and the milkmaid from Parkway? Had Francis Constantine played some part in the death of Lizzie Warren on the top of Hangman Hill on that fateful Sunday morning all those years ago?

11

New York

The shot rang out!

'Drop your weapons and put your hands up in the air!' shouted an unfamiliar voice.

'Damn it! Pinkertons!' exclaimed O'Callaghan.

Ravenscroft opened his eyes and looked across towards the entrance, where a group of men had just rushed into the room. Then there was a crash as O'Callaghan dropped the lantern, and a rushing of feet and shouting as the place was plunged into darkness and chaos.

'Grab hold of them, men! Don't let any of them get away!' instructed the first voice.

Ravenscroft strained to see what was going on in the room, but all he could make out in the gloom were groups of men fighting and crashing into each other as various cries and shouts rang out.

'Soon have you free, Mr Ravenscroft,' said the first voice, bending down and untying the rope as one or two lanterns were lit.

'Who are you?' stuttered Ravenscroft, finding that he was shaking with both relief and anxiety.

'Bill Richardson, Pinkerton agent at your service,' replied the man.

'I saw you in the boarding house. I remember we collided in the hallway,' said Ravenscroft, rubbing his wrists where the rope had bit into the flesh.

'Sure did.'

'You've been following me?'

'Sure have — Blackwell's Penitentiary, Macy's department store. You've been a busy man, Mr Ravenscroft.'

'But why?' asked Ravenscroft, standing up.

'Well, we've been after these fellows for years. We couldn't be sure that you weren't implicated in their crooked network, so the best thing we could do was keep you under observation.'

'I assure you that I was not involved in their affairs.'

'I can see that now. Sorry we couldn't rescue you before, but we were hoping you'd lead us to these crooks, as I'm sure you'll appreciate.'

'Well I am very glad you arrived just in time. Another second and I would have been dead. You were also on the *Etruria*, were you not?'

'Sure were. You were getting mighty close to O'Callaghan and his associates.'

'So it was you who sent me the warning note?'

'Guilty as charged,' laughed Richardson.

'You were travelling back from England. It must have been you who took those photographs from out of my drawer in Ledbury.'

'I guess you'll have to charge me with breaking and entering.'

'And you destroyed the photographic plates at Lancing's studio?'

'Yes. I must say I feel rather bad about that. Before you leave New York, I'll make a payment to the said gentleman, which you can give to him to cover the cost of the damage caused.'

'But why? Why did you take the photographs of Jacob? What were you trying to conceal?' asked Ravenscroft, still recovering from his ordeal.

'Well that's a long story. I suggest that after we've rounded up these villains, we repair to a little drinking establishment I know, where we can exchange information.'

'I could certainly do with a drink.'

'We've got Petters and Foy and most of the gang,' said a uniformed officer, breaking into the conversation.

'Good work, Captain. We'll be interested in what they've got to say for themselves back at the station. Where's O'Callaghan?'

'I'm afraid he's gone, Mr Richardson.'

'What do you mean, gone?' snapped the Pinkerton agent.

'He must have slipped out unnoticed in the dark, down the back stairway. I've sent two of my men after him. Hopefully they'll soon apprehend the felon.'

'Dash it! I shouldn't be so sure of that. O'Callaghan is a slippery character. I've been after him for years.'

'Sorry, Mr Richardson,' muttered the officer.

'Well there's nothing else for it. We'll be along later to the station to see what we can get out of these villains, after I've given poor Mr Ravenscroft here some liquid refreshment. I don't know, you English are always getting yourselves in trouble and expecting us Americans to come to your assistance,' joked Richardson. 'I wonder how many more times we'll have to do that in the years ahead.'

★   ★   ★

'Here, take a swig of that,' said Richardson, placing a glass before Ravenscroft.

'What is it?'

'Bourbon. It comes all the way from Kentucky. The finest American whisky.' Ravenscroft picked up the glass and swallowed some of its contents. 'It is certainly strong.'

'It can't be beaten.'

'Indeed. It seems, Mr Richardson, that I owe you a deep debt of gratitude for saving my life.'

'Think nothing of it,' replied the Pinkerton man, replenishing Ravenscroft's glass from the bottle on the table.

'I believe you may also have been instrumental in saving my wife from those criminals in Limehouse.'

'All part of the job.'

'If you hadn't rescued Lucy, I'm sure she would have been taken captive to one of their opium dens. It doesn't bear thinking about.'

'Always like to rescue a damsel in distress,' said Richardson with a smile before downing another glass.

'I believe it would be most beneficial to both of us if we shared our knowledge of this case,' suggested Ravenscroft.

'My very thoughts. You've heard of the Pinkertons?'

'Of course; America's leading detective agency.'

'We sure are. Founded by Alan Pinkerton in Chicago around 1850. Our motto is 'The eye never sleeps.' Once we have a man in our sights, we won't rest until he's brought to justice. Do you know there are more Pinkerton agents in America now than there are members of the American army?' boasted Richardson.

'There must be a great deal of crime over here.'

'There sure is!'

'Tell me all that you know about O'Callaghan.'

'He's one of the greatest villains to have ever walked this planet. The Pinkertons have been after him for at least ten years now, but every time we've gotten close to apprehending him, the man slips through our fingers. Petters and Foy are his main associates, but there are many others in the criminal fraternity. Their speciality is breaking into banks. Foy is an expert safe blower, whereas Petters is the strong man of the outfit. O'Callaghan is the brains, of course; he plans each robbery meticulously.

'They started out by raiding banks here in New York, but when things got too hot for them they went to other parts of America. There was a big job in 'Frisco three years back; before that there was one in New Orleans, and all the time O'Callaghan has been getting richer and richer. He lives in a fine house in Boston. They're pretty audacious as well. On their last job here they even dug a tunnel underneath the ground, which went from a nearby building right into the vaults of the bank.'

'A bit like 'The Read-Headed League',' interjected Ravenscroft.

'Red-Headed League?' asked a puzzled Richardson.

'Sorry, it's a story by one of our writers, Mr Arthur Conan Doyle. But if you know all this about O'Callaghan, why have you never been able to arrest him?'

'Because unfortunately he has a great many members of the police authorities in his pocket, and he also employs a very smart lawyer. Anyway, to resume, two years ago we learned that O'Callaghan had moved his activities across to your country.'

'Go on.'

'Last year there was a big robbery at one of the jeweller's in Bond Street in London. They got away with some very choice items by all accounts.'

'Yes, I remember reading about it at the time. No one was caught.'

'Exactly. Then there was a bank robbery in Birmingham. Foy blew the safe. We believe they got away with a stack of money and bonds that time, although the bank wasn't exactly forthcoming in regard to the true amount. They had their reputation to uphold.'

'That is understandable. Now tell me, where does the man Rockstone fit into all this?' asked Ravenscroft.

'Silas Rockstone is a complete charlatan and thief.'

'And is he an associate of O'Callaghan's?'

'Oh yes. They go back together a long way. They were in the Civil War together, although we can't be sure which side they supported, the Union or the Confederates, as they were often in the habit of faking their own deaths and selling armaments to both sides. They were as thick as two thieves. Why, they even courted the same woman, the infamous Kitty O'Mara, mistress of the famous Kentucky Casino.'

'So what was Rockstone doing in England?'

'We know that he left New York just over a year ago. Things were getting rather hot for him over here, and I guess he just wanted to go somewhere different until things had cooled down, or so we thought. But of course he was an important part of O'Callaghan's operation in England. Have another drink?'

'No, thank you,' replied Ravenscroft, feeling that the liquor was beginning to have its effect on him.

'We believe Rockstone committed a number of robberies in your country during the past year. He uses the travelling fair as his cover. As it moves around the country, Rockstone seeks out likely places to burgle; usually empty houses when the people are away — small country banks with out-of-date safes, that kind of thing. We believe he was stashing away the spoils, then passing them on later to his old friend O'Callaghan.'

'So the valuables he stole would eventually find their way to New York?'

'Precisely. If Rockstone tries to pawn or sell the stolen items in England, there's a chance they'd be identified and traced back to him; but of course in New York the valuables could be sold without any fear of that happening.'

'Very clever. But tell me, where does the man Jacob fit into all this?'

Richardson sat back in his chair and smiled. 'Jacob was a petty crook who joined up with Rockstone a couple of years ago before they went to England. What Rockstone didn't know, of course, is that Jacob was *our* man.'

'You mean Jacob was a Pinkerton agent?' asked a surprised Ravenscroft.

'Well not exactly. Two years ago he'd gotten himself into a lot of trouble here in New York, stealing from one or two high-class establishments. We caught him in the act, as they say, and we saw a wonderful opportunity opening up for us. So we did a deal with him. He'd get out of going to prison, and in exchange he'd work for us. We needed someone on the inside. So we suggested that he get friendly with Rockstone and become his accomplice. In time we hoped he'd lead us to O'Callaghan himself.'

'I see. And was that why you were in

England when Jacob was killed?'

'We hadn't heard anything from him since he'd arrived in your country, but we knew something big was probably about to take place. The agency decided to send me over there to find out what had happened. Unfortunately, I arrived in Ledbury three days too late. He was already dead by then.'

'So you think Rockstone found out that Jacob was working for the Pinkertons, and that's why he was killed?'

'It seems highly likely.'

'Why did you take the photographs of him and also destroy the negatives?'

'We believe in protecting the identity of our agents. We didn't want to run the risk that someone would come forward and claim to have recognised him. I learned that you were investigating the case, and that you'd sent your wife to London on some kind of errand, so that was why I decided to follow her that day.'

'It was fortunate that you did so.'

'What I couldn't understand, Mr Ravenscroft, is what your wife was doing visiting the Foundling Hospital, and then Mincing and Stricket.'

'I think it's time I told you about my own involvement in this case.'

'If you would, I'd be much obliged.'

During the next few minutes, Ravenscroft recounted how he and Crabb had recovered the locket from Rockstone and of its miniature inside, and how this had led him to the artist Louis Thermaine in Cirencester, and then to Maria Constantine at The Verzons, and how Lucy had learnt the woman's tragic story which in turn had taken her to London and himself to New York.

'So you think that this Thomas Temple could have been Jacob?' asked Richardson after he had listened intently to Ravenscroft's account.

'I don't honestly know whether I can answer that question. The last I heard was that Temple left Macy's store in 1885 and returned to England, but of course he may have remained in New York and changed his name to Jacob. Can you tell me anything about Jacob before you arrested him two years ago?'

'I'm afraid I can't help you much there. We knew that Jacob had been involved in his criminal activities in New York for at least a year before we arrested him in 1889.'

'So if he did go to England in 1885, he could well have returned to New York sometime before 1888?'

'That's possible. I'm sorry I can't be of any more help.'

'One more question, if you please.'

'Only one?' said Richardson, smiling.

'What were O'Callaghan and his associates doing on the *Etruria,* and why were you on the same ship? Although I think I know the answer to the second question.'

'As I said earlier, I was aware of your involvement in the case, and at that time believed that if I followed you, you might just provide me with the answers I was looking for. Then I was surprised that O'Callaghan, Petters and Foy were also on board. Clearly they were returning to their homeland because they now considered it safe to do so.'

'They could have met up with Rockstone before they left England.'

'Who no doubt passed over some of the valuables he'd stolen, although it's my belief that O'Callaghan wouldn't have been so foolish as to actually keep stolen goods in his possession. He couldn't run the risk of being apprehended by the authorities upon his return to New York. No, we believe that the jewels and other valuables were being transported from your country to New York through Mincing and Stricket. We netted quite a haul tonight in that warehouse.'

'I see. It would have been perfect cover. It would also explain why Thomas Temple was arrested for receiving stolen property. The gang could have been using Mincing and

Stricket for years to transport stolen valuables under cover to New York. That might explain why young Temple was arrested for receiving stolen goods.'

'Could well be,' Richardson agreed. 'Anyway, it's time we visited the police station to see what we can get out of those villains, Petters and Foy.'

Ravenscroft rose from his chair and followed the Pinkerton agent out of the room. Now at last he realised that the captured criminals might be able to provide him with the information he so desperately sought about the murder of Jacob, and the reasons why he had been killed.

⋆　⋆　⋆

'Now then, Petters, you'll no doubt be aware that your boss O'Callaghan has left you and your companions to accept all the blame,' said Richardson as he and Ravenscroft faced the criminal across the table in the dimly lit police room.

'I don't know what you're talking about,' muttered Petters.

'Twenty cardboard boxes found in the warehouse, containing numerous pieces of jewellery and other precious items, stolen from households in England and shipped across to here by Mincing and Stricket,' continued the Pink-erton agent, looking down at the sheet in front of him.

'I don't know what you're talking about,' repeated Petters arrogantly as he leaned back in his chair and drummed his fingers on the table.

'My colleague here saw you remove one of the parcels from the warehouse earlier today. You're in a great deal of trouble, Petters. Receiving and dealing in stolen goods, threatening to kill a police officer, burglary and theft — the list is endless. You're going to prison for a very long time. There's a rather draughty, uncomfortable cell on Blackwell's that's been reserved for you, and while you're there for the next fifteen years you can remember that your boss O'Callaghan will be living the high life in his nice cosy mansion in Boston. That doesn't sound quite right to me, does it, letting you and Foy take all the blame while he goes completely free?'

'So what? I don't give a damn.'

'You tell us what you know, and in return we might have a word with the authorities to see that you receive a lighter sentence,' said Richardson. 'That cell over at Blackwell's Penitentiary can be mighty cold and uncom-fortable at this time of the year. Fifteen years? I don't reckon you'll last beyond three, unless you go insane before then.'

Ravenscroft glanced across at the man and could see that beneath the bravado their quarry had a look of fear in his eyes.

'Tell me what you want to know,' said Petters after a long silence.

'Firstly, I want to know where O'Callaghan might be hiding,' Richardson said. 'You know all his old haunts. He must be somewhere here in New York.'

'No, I can't do that. If ever he found out I told you, my life would be over.'

'Then tell us about the Bond Street robbery in London,' said Richardson, changing tack as he looked down at his paper again.

'Yes, that was me.'

'Who was with you?'

'Foy and O'Callaghan.'

'What about the bank robbery in Birmingham?'

'Yes, that was me as well,' sighed Petters.

'Now we're getting somewhere. I take it you were also involved in the bank robberies in 'Frisco and New Orleans?' continued Richardson, anxious to press home his advantage.

'Yes,' muttered Petters in an almost inaudible whisper.

'I'm sorry, Mr Petters, but my colleague here didn't hear you.'

'Yes, yes,' replied the criminal irritably.

'When did you and O'Callaghan and Foy travel over to England?'

'I can't remember.'

'Try. We can check the passenger lists.'

'Six months ago.'

'What was the purpose of your visit there?'

'I'd rather not say.'

'Come now, Petters, this won't do. And just when things were going well for you. I'll ask you one more time — why did you go to England?'

'Things were getting hot for us here, after the Manhattan diamond break-in.'

'I *thought* O'Callaghan was behind that,' said Richardson with a degree of satisfaction.

'So we decided to lie low in England until things quieted down.'

'Did you see Rockstone whilst you were there?' interjected Ravenscroft.

'We met up with him in London. He told us he'd arranged for the valuables to be parcelled up and sent over to the warehouse here by Mincing and Stricket.'

'Was Jacob with Rockstone?'

'Who's Jacob?' replied Petters with a look of puzzlement on his face.

'Oh come now, Petters, you know who Jacob was,' said an annoyed Richardson, raising his voice.

'All right, all right. I'd met him once or twice in New York, two or three years ago.'

'That's better. Now was Jacob with Rockstone when you met him in London?' continued the Pinkerton detective.

'No.'

'But you knew that Jacob was working with Rockstone?' asked Ravenscroft, leaning forwards and looking Petters directly in the eyes.

'I had heard something about that.'

'You know that Jacob is dead?'

'No, I didn't.'

'We found him hanging from a branch on a hill near Malvern,' Ravenscroft told him.

'I didn't have anything to do with it,' protested Petters, showing a look of alarm.

'So you *did* know that Jacob had been killed?'

'No, not until you mentioned it just now.'

'Did Rockstone ask you to travel to Ledbury with Jacob and hang him up from a tree?'

'No! What is this? Where is this Ledbury, and this Malvern? I've never been to such places. I don't know what you're talking about,' pleaded Petters anxiously.

'Come on, Petters,' interrupted Richardson. 'If you didn't kill Jacob, then you know who did. Was it Foy who killed him, or O'Callaghan, or Rockstone himself?'

'I tell you, Mr Richardson, I don't know what you're talking about. I hardly knew this Jacob. I certainly never met him while we were in England. I'll confess to all the other robberies, but I never committed any murder. You know murder isn't my thing. I'd never hurt a fly. You must believe me!'

Ravenscroft looked at Richardson, who nodded in his direction. 'Take him away, officer,' said the Pinkerton man after a moment's silence had passed.

'I tell you, I know nothing about this murder! We were just in London looking at one or two jobs for the future,' said Petters as he was led away. 'You can't hang this on me.'

'You believe him, Mr Ravenscroft?' asked Richardson after the door had closed.

'Strangely, I do. I don't think O'Callaghan or his associates did kill Jacob.'

'I'm inclined to agree with you. Murder isn't one of O'Callaghan's usual crimes, although I must admit that he was going to make an exception concerning you. Rockstone must still be your most likely candidate.'

'Yes; that's why I need to return home as soon as possible. I want to secure the arrest of Silas Rockstone; and equally as importantly, I want to find out what happened to Temple after he left Macy's.'

'Then we'd better secure you a return berth on the next ship out of New York. I'm sorry we haven't been able to assist you in your search. It's been a pleasure meeting you, Mr Ravenscroft.'

'I return the compliment. Oh, there's one more thing you can do for me before I leave.'

'Just ask.'

'Do you know of anyone who sells butterflies?'

12

Herefordshire

'Well, Mrs Ravenscroft, that was certainly a clever idea of yours to go back to the Reading Rooms in Malvern, if I may so,' said Crabb as the trap made its way out towards The Verzons.

'I knew that it might prove worthwhile to see what else had been written in the local paper concerning the death of Lizzie Warren,' replied Lucy. 'I wonder why Francis Constantine attended her funeral.'

'Perhaps it was Mr Constantine who met Lizzie Warren on the hill that day,' suggested Crabb.

'You think he could have caused her death?'

'I don't know, Mrs Ravenscroft, but it will certainly be interesting to hear what he has to say about the matter.'

Crabb turned the trap into the courtyard of The Verzons, where they were met by the loud barking of a sheepdog.

'I think it might be better if we remain in the trap until someone comes,' said Lucy.

'That animal certainly doesn't appear to want us here,' replied Crabb, keeping a tight hold on the reins as the startled horse refused to stay still.

'Here, Brutus! Down!' shouted out a man's voice. The dog dropped to the ground and remained stationary.

'I wondered who had frightened him,' said Francis Constantine, emerging from one of the barns. 'Oh, it's you again, Constable Crabb. Where's Ravenscroft?'

'Away on business, sir,' answered Crabb, helping Lucy to step out of the trap. 'May I introduce Mrs Ravenscroft.'

'Mrs Ravenscroft,' acknowledged Constantine with a nod.

'I am pleased to make your acquaintance, Mr Constantine,' said Lucy.

'Well, Crabb what have you come here for?' asked Constantine bluntly. 'I thought we told you all about my sister's locket the last time you called.'

'It isn't about the death of Jacob,' said Crabb, observing that an anxious Maria Constantine was walking towards them.

'Good morning, Constable Crabb,' she said, drawing near.

'Good morning, Miss Constantine. May I introduce Mrs Ravenscroft,' said Crabb.

'I am pleased to make your acquaintance,

Miss Constantine,' said Lucy.

'Mrs Ravenscroft,' replied Maria. 'Perhaps you'd like to come indoors and take some refreshment with me whilst my brother talks with the constable.'

'That would be most kind of you, Miss Constantine,' said Lucy, following Maria into the house.

'Now then, Crabb, what's this all about?' asked Francis Constantine. 'I don't have time to indulge in idle chatter, as I'm on the way to feeding some of my sheep, so you'll have to walk with me into the fields.'

'Thank you, sir. I will not take up too much of your time.'

★ ★ ★

'Quickly!' said Maria, closing the door behind herself and Lucy. 'My brother mustn't know that we've met before today.'

'Of course; I understand.'

'You have news of my son?'

'I'm afraid not. My husband has gone to America, as I communicated to you in my letter. He should have arrived in New York several days ago. I am sure that if your son is still in New York, my husband will find him.'

'It's so strange that he left his employment with those people all those years ago. I wonder why?' asked an anxious Maria.

'Perhaps he was offered a better position. I'm sure my husband will return soon, and any news that he has obtained I will pass on to you by letter as soon as possible,' said Lucy, trying to sound as reassuring as she could.

'I do hope your husband is able to find my son. I could not bear to grow old without knowing what had happened to him,' said Maria, tears beginning to form in her eyes.

'I am sure all will be well. You must have the courage to wait a while longer.'

'I've already waited for over thirty years. It is imperative that my brother never finds out what happened all those years ago.'

'I understand. Maria, I want to ask you a question. Do you recall anyone by the name of Lizzie Warren?'

'Lizzie Warren? The name seems familiar. What has she to do with my son?'

'Lizzie Warren died in unfortunate circumstances on Hangman Hill nearly ten years ago,' replied Lucy, ignoring the question. 'She died as the result of a fall.'

'What a terrible thing to have happened; the poor girl. Yes, I do remember reading about the unfortunate incident in the newspaper at the time.'

'I have just been reading the newspaper

report of her funeral, which was held at Little Malvern Priory. Your brother was listed as one of the mourners. Can you think of any reason why he would have attended the interment?'

'I don't know. You must ask him.'

'I think Constable Crabb may be doing so now.'

'Yes, of course. I remember now. Francis was Lizzie Warren's godfather.'

'So your brother knew the family?'

'Yes, he must have done. It was all such a long time ago. I think my brother knew Stephen Warren. He was a tenant farmer near Eastnor. When Lizzie was born, Mr Warren asked Francis if he would be godfather to his daughter Lizzie. I remember Francis saying at the time that he hardly knew the man, but he felt that he couldn't refuse such a personal request.'

'I noticed that there were no Warrens recorded at the funeral service.'

'Yes, that would be correct. Warren's wife died when Lizzie was little more than an infant, and Stephen Warren died a few years later. There were no other children, I believe. It was quite a sad case. The farm was taken back. I don't know what happened to Lizzie.'

'She gained employment with a Mr Rostagon, a farmer out at Parkway.'

'I see. I suppose my brother must have read about her death and decided to pay his respects at her funeral, as her godfather. But I don't know why you want to know all this. How is it relevant to the search for my son?'

'We think that Jacob may have met Lizzie on the morning she was killed. They were possibly romantically attached.'

'I see. I think my brother and your colleague are returning. We must go back to them.'

'Yes. Thank you for the information relating to your brother and Lizzie Warren.'

'Please, as soon as you know something . . .' said Maria, her voice trailing off to a whisper as she opened the door into the yard.

'You can trust me, Miss Constantine.'

'Ah, there you are,' said Francis.

'Have you told Constable Crabb everything you know?' asked Maria with a smile.

'Nothing much to tell,' replied the landowner.

'Well, Miss Constantine, it has been a pleasure to meet you. Thank you for your hospitality,' said Lucy before climbing into the trap.

The brother and sister watched as the trap made its way out of the stable yard and onto the road.

'Well that was a complete waste of time,'

grumbled Francis. 'I can't see why that woman had to come out all the way here with that constable. It looks as though the police are now in the habit of sending their wives out when there are enquiries wanting to be made.'

★   ★   ★

On the journey back to Ledbury, Lucy related to Crabb all that had taken place inside The Verzons.

'So Francis Constantine was Lizzie Warren's godfather!' exclaimed the constable.

'Why are you so surprised, Tom? Did he not admit the same to you?' asked Lucy.

'No, he denied all knowledge of the girl. Said he had never heard of her, and that the newspaper report of him attending the funeral must have been erroneous.'

'That is strange. According to Maria Constantine, her brother was asked to become godfather to Lizzie. He apparently knew the Warrens, who were tenant farmers out Eastnor way. Both Lizzie's father and mother died when she was young. I wonder why Francis did not offer to take the child under his care and protection? Instead, poor Lizzie ended up working for Mr Rostagon at Parkway. It couldn't have been an easy life for her. I have no reason, however, to doubt that Maria Constantine was telling me the truth.'

'If that's so, Mrs Ravenscroft, why did Francis Constantine deny ever having known Lizzie Warren? Why did he not just tell me the truth? What is he hiding?'

★ ★ ★

Two days later, Crabb and Sergeant Morris found themselves mingling with the crowds at the autumn fair in the busy Herefordshire market town of Ross-on-Wye. Both men had relinquished their police uniforms and were casually attired in clothes that were more suited to farm labourers.

'Well, Constable Crabb, have you caught sight of this American Rockstone yet?' asked the older man.

'No, Sergeant. I recognise Walker over there, trying to separate those poor lads from their hard-earned wages. He's the owner of the fair. I'm sure that Rockstone must be here somewhere,' replied Crabb, pulling down his cap so that his features were hidden from view.

'Perhaps the man won't come back to the fair now that it has returned to Herefordshire,' suggested Morris. 'He must know that the police are still on the lookout for him.'

'I fear that I may have called you out on a worthless errand,' sighed a frustrated Crabb.

'Never mind, lad. We'll give it a few more minutes before we call off the search.'

'Quickly — move over here, Sergeant!' said Crabb suddenly, indicating that Morris should join him behind one of the stalls.

'You've seen him?'

'No, but that youth over there — the one wearing the blue trousers and a green hat pulled down over his face — he was with Rockstone. He was the lad in the crowd who professed to have undertaken Rockstone's miracle cure,' whispered Crabb.

'Well spotted, Constable.'

'I suggest we follow him. He may lead us to Rockstone.'

'Good thinking.'

As the youth moved away from the crowd and made his way down the main street of the town, Crabb and Morris followed on discreetly behind. 'He seems to be turning down that road at the bottom of the hill,' said the former.

'Better give him a few seconds. We don't want to frighten him.'

'Perhaps he's meeting up with Rockstone, and they're planning to break into one of the houses.'

After some moments had passed, the two

men turned the corner and were relieved to see the youth walking under the street lamps in the distance.

'He may be leaving the town,' said Morris, quickening his pace.

'Wait!' indicated Crabb. 'Look, he's meeting someone at the end of the road.'

'Is it your man Rockstone?'

'I can't see his features; it's too dark.'

'They appear to be conversing.'

'Now they've gone across to that house. There appears to be no one at home, as the place is in darkness.'

'I suppose the owners and the servants have all gone to the fair. Keep back, Constable Crabb! We must not be seen,' urged Morris. 'You were right, lad. They appear to be forcing open one of the front windows.'

The two policemen watched as the youth and the other man climbed in through the window and disappeared from view.

'Now we shall have them!' said Morris.

'What should we do, Sergeant?'

'Wait here until they come out. We'll catch them red-handed. No point following them inside; we'd have difficulty seeing our way from one room to another in the dark,' answered Morris.

'They could leave by another exit,' suggested Crabb.

'Good thinking, Constable. You remain here, and I'll make my way down the road and round to the back of the houses. If they come out before I return, blow your whistle, draw your truncheon and then arrest them.'

'Right, Sergeant.'

'On no account move away from here unless you hear my whistle. Is that understood?'

'Yes, Sergeant.'

'I'll be back before you know it,' said Morris, giving a friendly wink of the eye.

Crabb watched as his superior briskly walked past the group of joined houses and then disappeared from view.

As his eyes focused on the window where the men had just entered, Crabb's thoughts turned to the many previous occasions when he and Ravenscroft had found themselves in similar situations, watching and waiting for criminals to appear, and he could not help but recall those unfortunate times when things had gone wrong and their adversary had absconded before they had secured an arrest. There had been successes and failures over the years, but now Crabb was determined that this would be one occasion when his opponent would not escape police custody. If the mystery of Jacob's death was to be solved, then Rockstone must be apprehended at all costs.

The wait seemed endless. Perhaps he and Morris had been observed by Rockstone's accomplice? If so, then the criminals might well have decided to leave from the back of the property. But then, surely they would have encountered his colleague? If they had done so, Crabb reasoned, they could have attacked the policeman and rendered him unconscious before he had been able to raise the alarm. Morris had certainly been gone for a long time, and Crabb became increasingly uneasy that his colleague had not returned. He found his heart pounding and sweat running down his back. His inclination was to follow in the footsteps of the older policeman and see whether he had been injured, but Morris had been adamant that he was not to leave his station on any account, and that he was to remain vigilant and prepared for any eventuality.

Suddenly Crabb saw some distant movement from inside the room, and then the gradual opening of the window. He removed his truncheon and whistle from the inside pocket of his coat as first the youth, then his accomplice, stepped over the window ledge and into the road, the former carrying what appeared to be a large sack over his shoulder. Raising his whistle to his lips, Crabb let out three loud blasts before running across the road towards the two startled men.

'Quick, it's the law!' shouted the youth, dropping the bag on the pavement.

'Stay where you are!' instructed Crabb, brandishing his truncheon as he neared the two men. 'It is the police; there is no escape! Raise your hands!'

'All right, my friend,' replied the older man, complying with the request.

'Rockstone!' exclaimed Crabb, drawing nearer.

'Grab him, boss! There are two of us and only one of him,' shouted the youth, approaching Crabb in a menacing manner.

'I warn you, give yourselves up. There are more of us,' said Crabb, trying to sound as bold as he could.

'Oh, I think you're bluffing, my friend,' laughed Rockstone.

'Come on, boss!' yelled the youth, running head first into Crabb with such force that the winded policeman was knocked to the ground.

'Grab his truncheon,' instructed Rockstone as Crabb and his adversary wrestled on the cobblestones.

'I'll take out his eyes!' shouted the youth as Crabb suddenly felt the truncheon wrenched from his hand.

'I've got it!' shouted Rockstone, picking up the weapon.

'Hit him with it, boss!' yelled the youth.

As Crabb looked up, he could see Rockstone raising the truncheon above him.

'I wouldn't do that, sir, if I were you,' interjected a familiar voice.

Rockstone dropped the weapon and let out a cry of pain as Morris brought his truncheon forcefully across the man's legs. Crabb gained the upper hand on his opponent and pinned him to the ground as Rockstone writhed in agony on the pavement.

'Put the cuffs on him, Constable Crabb,' said Morris.

Crabb reached into his pocket, withdrew the cuffs and secured them round the youth's wrists.

'Now then, Mr Rockstone, are you going to come quietly, or would you like another dose of my truncheon?' asked Morris, standing over the outstretched American.

'Confound you, sir!' uttered Rockstone, slowly staggering to his feet and rubbing his leg.

Morris seized the showman's hands and clasped a pair of cuffs round his wrists.

'Thank you, Sergeant,' said Crabb, pulling the defeated youth to his feet.

'All in a day's work, Constable Crabb,' said

Morris with a smile.

'You can't arrest me, my man,' said Rockstone. 'I'm a citizen of the Americas.'

'I don't care whether you're the president of the United States or the archangel Gabriel; you and your friend here are coming along with us,' said Morris, taking hold of his captive's arm.

'I know you,' said Rockstone, staring at Crabb. 'You were at the fair in Ledbury, with that Ravenscroft.'

'Correct, sir. And, Mr Rockstone, I am pleased to make your acquaintance again. We've been after you for a very long time; a very long time indeed,' said Crabb.

13

At Sea

Ravenscroft stood on the promenade deck of the *Etruria*, looking down on the remaining passengers, who were eagerly making their way along the dockside and up onto the gangplank of the vessel that would shortly be departing on its transatlantic return trip to England. Many of his sailing companions were already waving handkerchiefs and hand-held flags at their loved ones gathered along the harbour side. A six-piece band was busily engaged in playing American melodies, as a number of porters carrying cases and trunks of all shapes and colours struggled to make their way on board the ship.

Ravenscroft reflected on the days he had spent in the great city, and the journey he had undertaken: the grimy interior of Ma Scrivens' Lodging House in Manhattan; the forlorn prison on Blackwell's Island; the opulence and splendour of Macy's Department Store in central New York; the desperate situation he had found himself in at the near-deserted warehouse of Mincing and Stricket, and his rescue there by Richardson the Pinkerton agent. Now as he stood looking out at the busy scene, he could not help but feel a little sad that the adventure was almost over, as well as being somewhat disappointed that despite all his efforts he had still not found Maria Constantine's missing son. Adding to his frustration was the fact that he was also no further forward in discovering who had murdered Jacob, and whether the dead man had once been Thomas Temple or whether they had been two different men. Perhaps a few days' quiet contemplation at sea would provide him with the opportunity to reflect on past events, and help him to see how he could proceed with the case when he returned home.

He was awakened rudely from his deliberations by a loud blast from the ship, indicating that its departure was imminent.

'Ravenscroft! Ravenscroft!' shouted a familiar voice.

He strained to see the owner of the cry amongst the waving crowds.

'Ravenscroft!' shouted the voice again.

'Here!' replied the detective, recognising Bill Richardson the Pinkerton agent, who was frantically engaged in waving a white envelope above his head.

Ravenscroft pushed his way quickly along the crowded deck full of passengers as he made his way towards the gangplank.

'All aboard! Last call!' shouted out a seaman, about to haul up the wooden staircase.

'Wait!' cried Ravenscroft. 'I must see that man. He has something for me.'

'Sorry, sir; no one else is allowed ashore.'

'But it is imperative; I must see that man. It is important police business.'

'Sorry sir, but — '

'Ravenscroft!' shouted Richardson, running up the gangway.

Ravenscroft brushed past the seaman and raced down to join Richardson.

'Here, take this!' instructed the Pinkerton man, thrusting the envelope into Ravenscroft's hand.

'Thank you. Have you caught O'Callaghan yet?'

'No, but it will only be a matter of time. Have a good voyage.'

'All aboard!' yelled out the seaman.

'Thank you for everything,' shouted Ravenscroft, quickly retracing his steps as he felt the wooden planks moving beneath his feet.

'See you in Herefordshire someday,' laughed the Pinkerton agent as he made his way back onto dry land.

Ravenscroft walked along the deck, eventually finding a place near the rail between the waving and cheering passengers, as the ship gave out another blast from its funnel. He looked out at the crowd on the harbour side and saw Richardson giving a brief wave in his direction before the Pinkerton agent disappeared in a sea of waving hands and flags.

As the ship pulled away from the harbour wall and the cheering crowds began to recede slowly into the distance, Ravenscroft looked out across the sea towards the large impressive statue jutting out into the waters, brandishing its torch of liberty and hope, and which seemed to him to be like some guardian and protector of its country. Then he made his way down towards his cabin.

*   *   *

Ravenscroft studied once more the three items on the bed before him, which he had removed from Richardson's envelope. The first was a hastily scribbled note from the Pinkerton man: 'Have just discovered that your man Temple shared a cell with Jacob during their time in Blackwell's!' The second was a copy of a passenger list dated 7 September, 1885, for a ship leaving New York for England, which included the name Thomas Temple. The third Ravenscroft recognised: it was the photograph of the dead Jacob, which Richardson had previously removed from his office in Ledbury.

So now he knew that Temple and Jacob were two different men!

The man whom he had found hanging on Hangman Hill had been the petty New York criminal, and not Maria Constantine's son. Temple and Jacob had evidently shared a cell together on the prison island all those years ago. Was that how Jacob had acquired Temple's locket? Had he stolen it from his companion one night when he had been asleep, or even taken it from him by force? He could not imagine that Temple would have given away his most prized possession.

Then there was the passenger list, which proved that when Temple had left Macy's he had indeed returned to England. But that had been six years ago. What had happened to Temple when he had landed in Liverpool? He had been able to trace the man's movements during his time in America, but now the inspector was faced with an even greater problem: discovering what had happened to Temple when he returned to England. But the more he thought about it, the more confident he was in the sad conclusion that his quest might go unresolved. At least he would be able to tell Maria Constantine that the dead man on Hangman Hill had not been her son.

It was fortunate that he now had the photograph of the dead Jacob, so that he could continue his enquiries when he returned to Ledbury. And there was always the hope that Crabb might have caught up with Rockstone during his absence, and that the murder would have been solved.

After dressing for dinner, Ravenscroft made his way to the second-class dining room, where he gave instructions to the waiter that he wished to dine alone. He had no inclination to be sociable that night, and after his previous experience on the outward journey now had no desire to be seated with another group of strangers. Allocated a corner seat, he spent the next hour eating, reading, and gazing out of the window at the people walking up and down on the deck.

'Would you like another cup of coffee, sir?' asked the waiter, breaking into the detective's thoughts.

'No, thank you.' As Ravenscroft began to gather his napkin, he suddenly caught sight of a familiar figure dressed in a long dark astrakhan overcoat passing swiftly by on the deck.

'Good God! It's O'Callaghan!' he exclaimed, rising from his seat quickly and nearly colliding with the waiter as he did so.

Ravenscroft ran across the dining room, much to the alarm of both diners and waiters, and out through the doors and onto the deck.

He looked frantically for the figure, but could see no one. Had O'Callaghan seen him and effected his escape?

He darted down the deck, pushing open doors as he did so, but there was no sign of his quarry. However, as he turned the corner of the promenade deck and found himself on the other side of the ship, he saw a familiar figure in the distance, and ran quickly towards him.

'So, O'Callaghan, we've caught you at last!' exclaimed Ravenscroft, grabbing the man's shoulder.

'I beg your pardon!' said the man indignantly.

'Forgive me, sir. I am so sorry. I mistook you for someone else,' stuttered Ravenscroft.

The man gave him a stern look of reproach before continuing his walk around the deck.

Ravenscroft let out a deep sigh, removed his spectacles and wiped them on his handkerchief. Had he really seen O'Callaghan, or had his memory played tricks on him? Surely the criminal would not have dared to escape his captors in New York by securing a berth on the same ship that had recently brought him to America?

During the next thirty minutes, Ravenscroft walked the many decks of the ship, desperately searching for the criminal in all the public rooms and corridors, but without success. Finally he made his way to the office in the centre of the ship.

'Good evening to you, sir. How may I be of assistance?' asked the polite young receptionist standing behind a counter.

'I wonder if I might look at the passenger list?' replied Ravenscroft.

'I'm sorry, sir, but that's not possible.'

'Oh? Why is that?'

'The company insists on the confidentiality of all its passengers.'

'I am a police officer, and I believe that one of your passengers may be a wanted criminal.'

'Really? If you'd care to wait here for a moment,' said the receptionist, before going over towards his older companion who had been busily writing further along the counter.

Ravenscroft shuffled uneasily as he watched the two men whispering intently together.

'I understand that you wish to see the passenger list, sir?' asked the senior receptionist, looking intently at Ravenscroft.

'Yes. I am an English police officer. I have reason to believe that a Mr O'Callaghan might be on board. He is a notorious criminal wanted by the New York police,' said Ravenscroft, feeling himself growing hot under his collar.

'As my colleague here has just informed you, sir, I am afraid that will not be possible.'

Ravenscroft took out his identity card and placed it on the counter. 'The New York police and the Pinkerton Detective Agency are both searching for this man, and I also have reason to believe that he may have been responsible for a murder committed recently in England.'

The senior receptionist looked at Ravenscroft, then at his companion, and then again at Ravenscroft.

'I appreciate that you can't let me see the passenger list, but at least if you could check the register yourself . . . ?' pleaded Ravenscroft.

'I suppose it will do no harm,' replied the receptionist, opening a large ledger that was on the counter. 'Callaghan, you said?'

'O'Callaghan,' corrected Ravenscroft.

The man ran his finger down the list of names. 'I'm sorry, but there's no one with that name travelling on this ship.'

'I see. Then perhaps he's travelling under another name.'

'That could be possible, sir, but maybe you were mistaken in regard to this passenger,' suggested the receptionist, adopting what Ravenscroft considered a superior manner.

'No, I am not mistaken.'

'Then I don't see how we can help you. All I can suggest is that if you see this man again, you call for assistance, and we'll apprehend him.'

'Yes. Thank you for your help,' sighed Ravenscroft before walking away.

He was sure that it had been O'Callaghan he had seen through the window, even if it had only been for a fraction of a second. It was obvious that the man was travelling under an assumed name. O'Callaghan was an experienced criminal. He would not have given his real name when he had embarked, knowing that the authorities in New York might still apprehend him; and if he had seen Ravenscroft through the dining-room window, then that would explain his sudden disappearance.

The *Etruria* had many cabins. Ravenscroft was sure that one of them contained the criminal mastermind; but he realised that neither he nor the ship's men could search every one of them. He would just have to wait until O'Callaghan made another appearance.

★ ★ ★

During the next few days, as the *Etruria* made its way across the Atlantic Ocean towards the port of Liverpool, Ravenscroft walked the various decks of the vessel, seeking out the American, but achieved no success.

Now on the night before the ship's arrival, he stood alone on the promenade deck, looking out to sea, wondering what the next day would bring and what news would be waiting for him upon his return to Ledbury. He could hear the distant sound of voices shouting and singing to the accompaniment of a piano. A refreshing breeze blew across his face as he saw the distant light from a passing ship in the far distance.

He was disturbed by the opening of a door at the end of the deck. A white-coated steward emerged, head bent low, humming a tune as he began earnestly to mop down the boards. Ravenscroft took out his pocket watch, observed that the time was approaching eleven, and decided that he would shortly retire so that he would be up early the next day to watch the passengers leave the ship. He was determined that O'Callaghan would not escape; and if the criminal did not disembark, he resolved that he would call upon the Liverpool police to make a detailed search of the vessel.

Suddenly he felt a sharp pain on the side of his head, and his vision clouded over as he found himself falling to the deck. He let out a loud groan and looked up to see a familiar face standing over him. 'O'Callaghan!' he muttered as the American grabbed his arms and roughly hauled him upright.

'Damn you, Ravenscroft! Did you think you could arrest me?'

Ravenscroft could feel the blood pouring down his face as his opponent pushed him up against the rails.

'You interfering fool!' growled O'Callaghan.

'Give yourself up, man. You won't get away with this.'

'Don't make me laugh!' replied O'Callaghan, angrily thrusting his features into Ravenscroft's face.

'My companions will be waiting for me in Liverpool. If I'm not there, they'll search this ship until they find you,' blurted out Ravenscroft as his adversary appeared to sway from side to side in the darkness.

'You English, always useless when it comes to defeat,' snarled O'Callaghan as he began to push Ravenscroft backwards over the edge of the rail.

'No!' cried the inspector, lashing out with his foot as he thrust himself forwards, seeking to grab his opponent's arms.

'I'll have you, Ravenscroft!' shouted O'Callaghan as the two men grappled with one another.

Ravenscroft knew that he was fighting for his life. He momentarily saw Lucy in the mist that was beginning to close in upon him, and made one last determined effort to break free from his adversary. The two men separated.

'Curse you!' yelled O'Callaghan, angrily rushing towards Ravenscroft as he sought to push the detective overboard.

Ravenscroft threw himself to one side of the deck as he felt the American rush past him. O'Callaghan let out a loud scream as he disappeared from view over the side of the ship.

Ravenscroft dragged himself to his feet and gazed at the waters below. 'Man overboard! Man overboard!' he shouted as he searched in the dark for any sign of O'Callaghan. As he sought to support himself by holding on to the rail, he heard the sound of running feet and anxious shouting. 'He . . . he . . . tried to kill me,' he stuttered, grasping the lapel of the officer he had spoken to previously.

He heard a loud splash as someone threw a life jacket over the side. 'Bring a light!' instructed the officer. 'You there, take care of this man.' Ravenscroft felt himself being supported by two men.

'It's no good, sir. He's gone!' said another voice.

'Look again, I tell you!' shouted the officer. 'Shine that light down there.'

'There's nothing, sir. He's gone.'

'Damn it!'

'Easy there,' added another voice assisting

Ravenscroft. 'Take it easy, sir. We'll soon have you attended to.'

As Ravenscroft was taken below decks and his wound cleaned and dressed, he realised that he had been fortunate to have survived the attack. O'Callaghan was now dead, that was a fact; but with the criminal's demise might also have gone the last opportunity of knowing who had killed Jacob.

14

Herefordshire

'You have a rather nasty bruise there,' said Lucy. 'Are you sure you wouldn't like me to bathe it again for you?'

It was later the next day, and the detective, his wife and Crabb were sitting round the dining table in the small house in Church Lane in Ledbury, having each recounted their experiences during the past few weeks.

'No thank you, my dear. The ship's doctor managed to attend to me after my encounter with O'Callaghan, and I felt much better this morning after a good night's sleep.'

'You had a lucky escape, sir,' said Crabb sympathetically.

'Being nearly killed twice in seven days must be somewhat of a record even for you,' added Lucy light-heartedly.

'Yes. Do you know, when that villain was about to throw me over the side, it was your face, my dear, that suddenly appeared before me. And I think it was that which gave me the strength to not let him get the better of me. It was a pity that I was unable to question the man. I'm sure he knew both Jacob and Temple, and that he was probably involved in the former's death.'

'Well at least you now know that Jacob and Temple were not the same man, and that Maria Constantine's son must still be alive,' said Lucy.

'We cannot be sure of that. All we know is that he returned to England sometime towards the end of 1885. Where he went to after that is anyone's guess.'

'At least it will be some consolation for Miss Constantine,' added Lucy. 'I will write to her later today.'

'So Jacob stole the locket from Temple whilst they were in prison?' asked Crabb.

'You would have thought he'd have sold it at the first opportunity, instead of keeping it,' said Lucy.

'Yes, but he evidently took a liking to it and decided to keep it. It was fortunate for us that he did so, and that we compelled Rockstone to hand it over to us. Had he not done, or had Jacob disposed of it earlier, we wouldn't have been able to progress further with our investigations. It's been a long trail that has taken us from Cirencester, to The Verzons, to the Foundling Hospital and Mincing and Stricket in London, and across the Atlantic Ocean to New York, but it's still frustrating that after all that we are no further forward with discovering either who murdered Jacob, or where the elusive Thomas Temple is now.'

'At least we have Rockstone and his accomplice in custody,' said Crabb.

'Indeed we have; and I must congratulate you, Tom, on an excellent piece of detective work during my absence. To realise that Rockstone was using the fair as cover for his criminal activities was clever, and you and Sergeant Morris did an excellent job in arresting the man. Have you been able to obtain any information from him?'

'His accomplice has admitted all the burglaries we knew about, and a few other ones as well; but Rockstone himself is denying everything, including the hanging of Jacob,' replied Crabb.

'Perhaps now that we know he is a former associate of O'Callaghan's, he might be more forthcoming with his answers. But it seems that I must also thank you as well, my dear, for your uncovering of the death of Lizzie Warren. I should perhaps go away more often and leave the solving of crimes to you and Tom here,' Ravenscroft joked.

'We are pleased to assist you at any time,' laughed Lucy.

'From what you've told me, it seems that Lizzie Warren may have died as the result of some kind of assault on Hangman Hill, rather than her death being caused by her falling and hitting her head on a rock. If that was the case, then Jacob could have killed her. We know that she was seeing him at that time. They could have quarrelled, then he pushed her, and she died. I guess we'll never know the exact details of the incident, as both parties are now dead; but we do know that Jacob must have left for America shortly afterwards, and that when he returned to this country with Rockstone and learnt that the fair was journeying to Hereford, he was obviously very reluctant to travel there.'

'In case someone recognised him,' suggested Lucy.

'Exactly. And clearly someone did, for he was taken captive to Hangman Hill and strung up from one of the trees there, at exactly the same place where Lizzie Warren had been killed all those years before.'

'Someone was seeking revenge for Lizzie Warren's death?' interjected Crabb.

'Precisely. But who would have wanted him dead? You mentioned that Francis Constantine was Lizzie Warren's godfather?'

'But surely he would not have committed the crime,' offered Lucy.

'He denied knowing Lizzie Warren when I questioned him,' said Crabb.

'I know, Tom, but I still can't see him as the murderer,' added Lucy.

'Then there's this farmer, Rostagon, who employed Lizzie. Perhaps he had been fond of her and wanted revenge on her assailant.'

'That could be a possibility. He certainly struck me as being a rather unpleasant man,' said Lucy.

'He was very abrupt, and seemed very disinterested in what we had to say,' added Crabb.

'You say that there was also a young man working on the farm?'

'Michael Sangster,' said Crabb.

'Do you think he could have been romantically attached to Lizzie Warren?' asked Ravenscroft.

'It could have been the case, sir,' answered Crabb.

'So he could have been holding a grudge against Jacob for Lizzie's death; and years later when he saw Jacob at the fair in Hereford, he decided to take the law into his own hands?'

'So we have Constantine, Rostagon and Sangster, any one of whom could have killed Jacob,' said Crabb.

'Or any combination of them, for I believe it may have taken two men to have hung Jacob from that tree. However, we also have Rockstone as a possible suspect. He could have killed Jacob,' said Ravenscroft.

'But why?' asked Lucy.

'Because the two men had a falling out, or Jacob was threatening to expose Rockstone to the authorities,' suggested Ravenscroft.

'Yes, but if that was so, why take him out to Hangman Hill to end his life?' continued Lucy.

'To make us believe that Jacob's death was some kind of revenge killing. Jacob could have told Rockstone all about the events on the hill when Lizzie died, and Rockstone then saw how he could kill Jacob and make it look as though someone else had committed the crime. I think we're dealing with a very clever man. You say, Tom, that Rockstone is still in custody?'

'Yes,' answered Crabb. 'Both he and his accomplice are at Hereford police station.'

'Then first thing tomorrow morning we'll travel over to Hereford. Now that O'Callaghan is dead, Rockstone might be more inclined to confess his sins.'

★ ★ ★

'Good morning to you, Sergeant Morris,' said Ravenscroft as he and Crabb entered the police station in Hereford the following morning.

'Good morning to you, Inspector,' replied the policeman, looking at the bruise on the side of Ravenscroft's head. 'It is good to see that you've returned safely. How did you find New York, sir?'

'Fascinating and dangerous. But it seems that you and Constable Crabb have been especially busy during my absence.'

'Indeed we have, sir. We have the villains in the cells now. The Rockstone fellow is saying nothing; but the other one, the young lad, has admitted everything.'

'Excellent. Perhaps you'd be kind enough to bring Rockstone up to the interview room, Sergeant.'

'Certainly, sir.'

Ravenscroft and Crabb made their way to the airless grey room at the back of the station. 'Now let's see what the American has to say for himself,' said Ravenscroft as he sat on a chair behind a small desk.

'You still think he killed Jacob?' asked Crabb.

'I don't know, but I mean to find out.'

The door opened and the handcuffed American and Sergeant Morris entered the room. 'Ah, Inspector Ravenscroft, I see,' said Rockstone with a smile.

'Take a seat, Mr Rockstone. I think we can dispense with the handcuffs, Morris. I am confident that our prisoner won't be going anywhere for quite a long time, unless it's to the nearest prison.'

'You don't have anything on me, Mr Ravenscroft,' laughed Rockstone as the policeman removed the cuffs.

'How would you explain your breaking and entering in Ross-on-Wye?'

'A misunderstanding, I can assure you,' replied Rockstone as he sat in the chair facing Ravenscroft.

'That isn't what your accomplice has told us. He has confessed to everything; all the break-ins and robberies over the past few months. There was quite a long list of them. He'll testify against you at your trial, no doubt in a futile attempt to save his own skin.'

'The boy is a romantic. He knows nothing,' said Rockstone in a carefree manner.

'Is that so? I can assure you that we can match the dates of at least ten robberies with the places where the fair was situated. We know that as you went round the towns and villages, putting up posters advertising the fair, you and your accomplice were on the lookout for suitable properties you could later break into.'

'A mere coincidence; that is all I can say.'

'It would be in your interest to tell us

where you've hidden all the items you appropriated.'

'I don't know what you're talking about. I'm afraid I can't help you, Inspector, as I have not taken anything from anyone's house,' replied a confident Rockstone, leaning back in his chair.

'Come now, Mr Rockstone; this won't do at all. We know that you and Jacob, and then you and the young lad we have in the cells, burgled all those houses. We also know that you then made up parcels of the stolen items, which you shipped to your associates in New York, using the services of Mincing and Stricket of Limehouse in London.'

'I'm afraid I still don't know what you're talking about. I've never heard of those people in London.'

'You may be interested to know, Mr Rockstone, that I've just returned from New York.'

'Is that where you acquired that bruise? New York can be a dangerous place for the unwary.'

'I was present when the police authorities and Pinkerton agents raided Mincing and Stricket's warehouse in New York. We found some interesting parcels there. Furthermore, your associates O'Callaghan, Foy and Petters were also found there.'

'I've never heard of these people,' said Rockstone, though Ravenscroft thought he saw a slight chink beginning to appear in his suspect's armour.

'Foy and Petters are now in police custody in New York. They've told us everything concerning your activities in this country. They've provided us with quite a detailed account. I am afraid you'll be in prison here for a very long time.'

'You have only their word for all this nonsense,' replied a defiant Rockstone.

'Your former associate O'Callaghan managed to escape. He tried to throw me overboard on the return journey to England, but unfortunately for him, he lost his footing and fell into the sea. I have to tell you that O'Callaghan has now been consigned to the depths of the Atlantic Ocean. He won't be able to help you in the future.'

'How unfortunate for him,' said Rockstone. Ravenscroft thought he observed a brief smile crossing the American's face.

'So you see, Mr Rockstone, we have the confessions of Foy and Petters, and the young lad in the cells. I'm afraid it's all over for you,' said Ravenscroft, trying to sound as confident as he could.

'You can't send me to prison. I'm a citizen of the United States of America.'

'I can assure you that many of your countrymen who have committed crimes in this country are now wasting away in English prisons. They are all alone and face the prospect of never seeing either their homeland or their loved ones ever again. Prison can be a very lonely, desperate place. Many of the prisoners never make it. Some go mad, while others commit suicide or die from maltreatment and disease, or are killed by other inmates.'

'All right!' interrupted Rockstone, banging his fist down hard on the table. 'You've made your point. You don't need to go on, man.'

'Then you admit to these crimes?' said Ravenscroft, leaning forward across the table.

Rockstone said nothing as he averted his eyes from Ravenscroft's stare.

'Then of course there's the matter of selling worthless pills and potions to innocent people,' continued Ravenscroft. 'That should add on a few years.'

'My remedies bring great benefits.'

'However, I am not really interested in all these burglaries and fake medicines. No, what really interests me is the death of your former assistant, Jacob.'

'I've told you all I know about Jacob.'

'Then you had better tell me it all over again,' emphasised Ravenscroft.

'I told you I met Jacob in New York. He was looking for work. I suggested he become my assistant. He accepted my offer. A few months later we came across to your country and joined Mr Walker's Travelling Fair,' sighed the American.

'And?'

'And what?'

'Why did you decide to kill him?'

'That's ridiculous. I had nothing to do with Jacob's demise. As I told you previously, Jacob was afraid to come back to Herefordshire.'

'Why was he afraid to return here?'

'I don't know. He never explained why.'

'I find that difficult to believe. Your colleague tells you that he does not wish to return to his home county, and you just accept what he says. You never thought to enquire further as to the reason?'

'No.'

'Well I'm afraid I don't believe you. I think Jacob told you how he killed Lizzie Warren on Hangman Hill all those years ago, and that you saw it as the perfect opportunity to be rid of a man who you thought was about to betray you to the authorities,' said Ravenscroft forcefully.

'This is all nonsense,' laughed Rockstone. 'Who is this Lizzie Warren? No doubt you'll say that I killed her as well.'

'Lizzie Warren was an innocent young woman who was murdered on Hangman Hill some ten years ago.'

'Well I was in New York then.'

'Nevertheless, you killed Jacob and hung him from that tree on top of that hill.'

'Look, Ravenscroft, this is all nonsense, utter nonsense. If I'd wanted to kill Jacob, I would've buried him under six feet of earth, where you or anyone else would never have found him. I'll take the blame for the robberies, but you sure as hell are not setting me up with a murder charge!'

'It's no use denying it, Rockstone. I believe you killed Jacob, after which you told us that fabricated story about how he didn't wish to return to Herefordshire. I'm going to make sure that you hang for this hideous crime.'

'No, no! You've got it all wrong!'

'I don't think so. You'll hang, Rockstone.'

'All right! I'll tell you the truth.' The bluster had completely disappeared from Rockstone's manner, and Ravenscroft could see fear in the man's eyes.

'Go on,' said the inspector, leaning back in his seat with some satisfaction.

'Jacob told me that he and this Lizzie Warren were lovers. They met in the hills on that Sunday. He said they argued, she became angry, he pushed her away and she fell, hitting her head on one of the rocks. He could see she was dead. Apparently he then panicked and ran away. When the body was recovered, suspicion fell on him, so he left the country in a hurry and went across to New York. When he knew that the fair was going to Hereford, he said he didn't wish to go there. He said there were powerful men who lived there, who if they recognised him would seek revenge for his part in the girl's death. That's all I know.'

'I see. Did Jacob say who these powerful men were?'

'No, that was all he said. Just that they were powerful men who would want revenge.'

'It's a pity he didn't tell you anything more.'

'Look, I'm sorry I can't help you further, Ravenscroft, but what I'm telling you is the truth. I never laid a hand on poor Jacob. I told him that it was all nonsense; that the people he alluded to were probably all dead or had long forgotten what had happened. He seemed to accept what I said, but then of course we came to Hereford and that was the last I saw of him. I suppose I should have taken him more seriously at the time. I had no idea that someone was going to hang him from a tree.'

Ravenscroft looked intently at his suspect for a moment before turning towards Sergeant Morris. 'Take Mr Rockstone back to his cell.'

'I'm telling you the truth, Ravenscroft. I did not kill Jacob. It was one of those men. You have to believe me!' protested Rockstone as Morris hauled his prisoner to his feet.

'Morris, take him away. We may need to have words with you later, Mr Rockstone,' said Ravenscroft, turning away.

'What will happen to me?' asked Rockstone as he was led towards the door.

'You'll stand trial on multiple counts of breaking and entering, burglary, and deceiving the public. Take him away, Sergeant Morris.'

'So you believe me about Jacob?' pleaded Rockstone.

Ravenscroft said nothing as Morris and Rockstone left the room.

'You believe him, sir?' asked Crabb once the door had closed.

'I think he was telling us the truth, but I cannot be absolutely sure. Our American is a very clever and astute character, I have no doubt. He could have invented this story about these 'powerful men' who were interested in taking revenge on poor Jacob in an attempt to draw us away from what

285

actually happened. If Rockstone's account is true, then it's very annoying that Jacob didn't tell him who those men were. Damn it, Tom, why is it that our lives do not become any easier? Who were these 'powerful men'? Rostagon? Sangster? Francis Constantine? Or was he referring to someone else we are yet to learn about?'

'There's someone else to consider,' said Crabb.

'Go on,' urged Ravenscroft.

'What about Thomas Temple? He shared a cell with Jacob whilst both men were in New York. We know that Jacob stole Temple's locket.'

'You think that Temple could have seen Jacob in Hereford, recognised him, abducted him and murdered him? It's a possibility of course, but would a man do all that because of a locket?' said Ravenscroft, thinking out loud.

'He was very attached to the keepsake. It contained the portrait of the mother he'd never known. He had grown up with it, and it was his only link with the past.'

'Yes, but Jacob didn't have the locket on him at the time of his death. If Temple wanted it back, surely he would have compelled Jacob to lead him to where it was, if it meant that much to him. No; sorry Tom, but I just don't believe that Temple killed Jacob. Anyway, we don't know where Temple is now. We do know that he returned to England six years ago, but what happened to him after that remains a mystery.'

'Miss Constantine will be sad that we haven't found her son.'

'I think we've done all that we can in that quarter. Just now, I think we need to turn our attention towards Lizzie Warren. Tom, whereabouts is the original police file on her death?'

'Back at the station in Ledbury. I managed to get it sent over from headquarters.'

'Then I think we should return there. But first I must instruct Sergeant Morris to proceed with the prosecutions of Rockstone and his accomplice.'

★ ★ ★

Ravenscroft sat in silence, reading the case notes on Lizzie Warren's death, while Crabb busied himself tidying the books and papers on the shelves.

'It tells us nothing!' Ravenscroft sighed as he flung the file onto the table. 'Accidental death caused by hitting her head on a rock as she fell. No other signs of violence. You say you've spoken with this former Inspector Robinson?'

'Yes, sir, and he confirmed what you've just said,' replied Crabb.

'Not a very detailed report. He interviewed both Rostagon and Sangster; that is all. There's no mention of Jacob. It's almost as though Robinson had made up his mind right from the beginning of the investigation as to the cause of death. Perhaps I need to ask him some more questions.'

'What shall we do after that, sir?'

'Go and see Rostagon and Sangster again.' Ravenscroft suddenly sat upright in his chair. 'But . . .'

'Yes, sir?'

'Tom, we may have been looking at this case from the wrong angle. Perhaps we should have been paying more attention to investigating Lizzie Warren's death instead of following the Jacob line of enquiry. I believe that when Mrs Ravenscroft read the newspaper report into Lizzie Warren's funeral, she discovered that the girl had been buried without any relations being present.'

'Yes, sir. We understand that both the mother and the father died before Lizzie, and that she had no brothers or sisters.'

'Where is Lizzie Warren buried?'

'Little Malvern Priory Church, I believe.'

'I wonder why they chose to bury her there of all places. You would have thought she'd be interred at Parkway where she worked, or at some other local church.'

'Perhaps her parents were also buried at Little Malvern.'

'You could be right, Tom. I think we should visit Little Malvern. Sometimes churchyards can reveal secrets about the living as well as the dead.'

★ ★ ★

Ravenscroft opened the old wooden gate that led into the churchyard of Little Malvern Priory. 'See if you can find Lizzie Warren's grave. Someone may have put up a stone for her. I'll take this side,' suggested Ravenscroft.

The two detectives made their way amongst the rows of headstones, reading the inscriptions as they did so.

'Here we are, sir,' called Crabb after a few minutes had elapsed.

'What does the inscription say?' asked Ravenscroft, joining his companion.

'Not much, sir. It just gives the name Lizzie Warren and the dates of her birth and death.'

'Is there nothing more?'

'No, sir. The stone doesn't even include the name of the stonemason who carved the inscription.'

'That is rather unhelpful. Nevertheless,

someone must have paid for this stone.'

'Francis Constantine? He was her godfather, after all, and we know he attended the funeral.'

'That is possible.'

'It's not much to show for a life, is it?' Ravenscroft and Crabb quickly turned round to see that the words had been spoken by a young man dressed in clerical attire.

'Indeed not,' said Ravenscroft. 'I take it that you are the vicar here at Little Malvern?'

'Alas, no; I am only the curate. Francis Davis. Can I be of any assistance to you gentlemen?'

'I hope so, Mr Davis. My name is Detective Inspector Ravenscroft, and this is my associate Constable Crabb. We've been investigating the death of the man found hanging on Hangman Hill.'

'Oh yes, I remember reading about it in the local newspaper. It was a terrible business. He's buried over there,' said the clergyman, pointing across the churchyard. 'There is no stone, only a simple wooden cross.'

'Indeed. But what concerns us at the moment is the girl here, Lizzie Warren. She also died on the hill some ten years ago.'

'I have heard of the event, but of course I wasn't at Malvern then. I have only been curate here for the past year or so.'

'I thought I hadn't seen you before,' said Crabb.

'This is only my second position since I joined the church five years ago.'

'Oh? Where were you before you came here, Mr Davis?' asked Ravenscroft.

'After being ordained, I was a curate in Dudley.'

'You must find this quite a change.'

'Indeed. It is so much more peaceful here. I wouldn't wish to be anywhere else,' said the clergyman, giving a broad smile.

'I wonder if we might trouble you to look at the church records?' asked Ravenscroft, returning to the matter at hand.

'Certainly,' replied the young man. 'If you'd care to follow me inside, gentlemen, I will be glad to show them to you.'

Ravenscroft and Crabb followed the clergyman into the interior of the church.

'The parish registers are kept in this oak chest here,' said the curate, pointing to the piece of furniture in the corner. 'I'll bring them over to you at the table.'

Ravenscroft and Crabb waited as the chest was unlocked and the old volumes brought over to them.

'Perhaps we could start with the burial entry for Lizzie Warren,' suggested Ravenscroft.

The clergyman opened one of the volumes and turned over the pages.

'Yes, there we are. Name, occupation, address, and date of burial,' said Ravenscroft, examining the entry. 'There is nothing unusual there. I believe that Lizzie Warren may also have been baptized here. I wonder if we could look at the records for twenty-one years before this date.'

The curate reached for another volume and again turned the pages. 'Ah, I think this may be what you are looking for, Inspector.'

'Lizzie Warren, baptised September 10th, daughter of Stephen Warren and his wife Mary,' said Ravenscroft, reading the entry aloud. 'We believe that Lizzie had no brothers or sisters?'

'We can go through the pages covering the years before and after that date,' suggested the curate.

Ravenscroft searched through the register. 'No, there are no further entries, so there would appear to be no siblings. I wonder if Lizzie's parents were also married here in this church. If Lizzie was born in early 1860, we would need to look for the years preceding that date.'

The clergyman placed a larger volume on the table and turned over the pages.

'Yes, here we are. Marriage of Stephen

Warren and Mary — Good lord!' exclaimed Ravenscroft, pointing at the entry.

'What is it, sir?' asked Crabb.

'See here, Tom,' indicated Ravenscroft. 'Do you see Mary Warren's maiden name?'

'Yes, sir.'

'This puts a new complexion on the case. Let's return to Lizzie Warren's grave. I wouldn't be surprised if we found some graves nearby of people with the same family name as this. Thank you, Mr Davis; you've been most helpful to us.'

Ravenscroft and Crabb quickly made their way out of the small church and returned to Lizzie Warren's grave.

'It's just as I thought!' exclaimed Ravenscroft. 'See the name on this stone next to Lizzie's?'

'It's the same family name on this one as well, sir,' said Crabb.

'We should have come here earlier. Lizzie was buried amongst her ancestors. How stupid we have been. I see it all now. Now we know not only who killed Jacob, but also why. It's time we paid a visit to our murderer.'

15

Herefordshire

Ravenscroft alighted from the trap outside the small cottage at Eastnor and walked up the garden path, closely followed by Crabb. As they neared the door, it was opened by an elderly grey-haired man.

'Caleb Robinson?' said Ravenscroft.

'Huh? I thought ye would be back.'

'May we come in?'

'If ye must.'

'I have to tell you that we know all about Lizzie Warren. Her mother was Mary Robinson — your sister, I believe. Lizzie Warren was your niece.'

'It took you a long time to work that out,' muttered the old man.

'It was you who saw Jacob at the fair in Hereford, and who returned the following night with your accomplice. Together you captured Jacob, bought him out here to Hangman Hill, and strung him up there from one of the trees. Then, when you were sure he was dead, you walked down to the inn and said you had found the body on your walk in the hills. It was also very clever of you to tell us that fanciful story of the horseman in the wood, in the hope that it would throw us off the scent. Your big mistake was not searching the lining of Jacob's coat. Everything we've learnt about this case came from that one small box of pills,' said Ravenscroft.

'Jacob got what was coming to him. He killed our beautiful Lizzie that morning on the hill. She didn't deserve to die. She were an innocent young lass until she met that awful man. He violated her and then he killed her. He escaped justice by running off to America, but I knew it were him when I saw him at that fair in Hereford that night. He deserved everything that were coming to him. I ain't sorry for what we did.'

'Lizzie Warren died as the result of an accident,' said Crabb.

'Accident? How do you know that? No, he killed her, and that's no mistake.'

'You cannot take the law into your own hands,' said Ravenscroft.

'The law!' growled Robinson. 'The law didn't help to bring justice for our Lizzie.'

'Crabb, put the cuffs on him.'

'I don't cares what will happen to me now. I'm an old man. Jacob paid for what he did to our Lizzie.'

'You will hang, just as poor Jacob hung,'

said Ravenscroft. 'Perhaps the hangman will show greater consideration towards you than you displayed towards Jacob. I also know who your accomplice was. We have him in custody now. He has told us everything.'

Robinson laughed. 'So you got Alfred as well. He won't tell you anything.'

Ravenscroft looked at Crabb. 'Alfred Robinson, the former police inspector at Malvern, who carried out the investigation into Lizzie Warren's death. He's your brother, I believe. I wonder, was it you or Alfred who placed the rope around Jacob's neck?'

'That's for you to find out,' retorted Robinson.

'It was your brother who found out that Lizzie had arranged to meet Jacob that morning on Hangman Hill, but he made no mention in his report that Jacob might have been responsible for her death. That was because he knew that the police authorities had no evidence against him. But before you and Alfred could take the law into your own hands, Jacob left the county in a hurry and went to America.'

'You knows it all, don't you. Clever, ain't you,' muttered the handcuffed man.

'Your brother was arrested two hours ago. He denied all knowledge of the murder of Jacob. However, you have just now confirmed his guilt. Both of you will stand trial for the murder of Jacob. Take him to the trap, Tom.'

* ★ *

'They will both hang of course,' said Ravenscroft as he and Lucy sat at the breakfast table the following morning.

'What a terrible thing to have done,' remarked Lucy. 'Poor Jacob.'

'Yes; and if it hadn't been for you, my dear, justice would never have been done. It was clever of you to go to the Reading Rooms in Malvern and look through past issues of the local newspaper to see if there had been any previous crimes committed on Hangman Hill. It was the account of Lizzie Warren's death that provided us with the information we needed to solve this case. Tom and I had given all our attention to the dead man and finding that scoundrel Rockstone. You should have been a detective.'

'Are there any female detectives in the police force?' asked Lucy.

'I don't know of any. Perhaps I should put your name forward,' laughed Ravenscroft.

'I have more than enough to occupy my time here, thank you, looking after two children and running this house.'

'And a very good job you make of it as

well, my dear. I suppose the ironic thing about this case was that the murderer was standing right by my side at the start of our enquiries, when we found Jacob on Hangman Hill, and we did not see that; although when I finally read Alfred Robinson's report into the death of Lizzie Warren, my suspicions were aroused. There was hardly any detail in the policeman's report, and he seemed anxious to end his investigation as soon as possible. I knew then that the answer might just lie in Little Malvern churchyard, where Lizzie was buried. When we returned to look at her grave, we could see that there were other stones nearby belonging to members of the Robinson family.'

'Well I am pleased that the case has come to a satisfactory conclusion.'

'But not for Maria Constantine. We still haven't found her son, despite my travelling halfway round the world in an attempt to do so.'

'You tried your hardest, Samuel. It must be some consolation to her that you were able to tell her about how her son was looked after by the Foundling Hospital, and how he secured that position at Mincing and Stricket in London, and then went to America.'

'Where he ended up in prison.'

'Only for a short while, before he was taken

on at Macy's. They must have thought highly of him.'

'Then he terminated his employment and came back to England.'

'I wonder why he decided to leave New York. Macy's does sound rather splendid, from the description you gave of it, and I do so like that silk shawl that you brought back for me. It was so kind of you.'

'I'm pleased you liked it,' said Ravenscroft with a smile before picking up his newspaper and resuming his reading.

'Samuel, I don't suppose you still have that locket?' said Lucy, looking up from her sewing.

'As a matter of fact I have,' replied Ravenscroft, reaching into his pocket. 'I've taken this locket halfway round the world with me, but now I suppose I must return it to Miss Constantine.'

'May I have another look at it? I haven't seen it since that night when you acquired it from Rockstone, and I should just like one further look at it before you give it back.'

'Here you are, my dear,' said Ravenscroft, passing over the item to his wife.

'It is such a beautiful portrait, and so well executed. I can see the resemblance quite clearly. Although it was painted by that Frenchman some thirty years ago, you would still know that it was Maria Constantine if you saw her today. The nose, and mouth, and that look in the eyes,' said Lucy, studying the miniature.

'Yes, I recognised the sitter as soon as I saw her.'

'Excuse me, sir. Ma'am. The morning post has just arrived,' said the maid, entering the room.

'Thank you, Susan,' said Lucy.

'A letter from America; must be from Richardson the Pinkerton agent I told you about,' said Ravenscroft, examining the envelope. 'I must write to him and tell him what happened to O'Callaghan.'

'How exciting.'

Ravenscroft opened the letter and read aloud its contents.

Ravenscroft,

Thought you might be interested in receiving the enclosed photograph.

After your departure yesterday, I paid a visit to Macy's — my brother-in-law is the senior clerk there. He made another search through the archives, and we found the enclosed photograph. It shows the staff members of the china department posing for the camera. I then asked around, and one or two of the people remembered your Thomas Temple. Apparently he is the second man in the back row.

I hope this is of some assistance to you.

Good luck,

Bill Richardson.

'That is most fortunate,' said Lucy.

'Where's the magnifying glass?' asked Ravenscroft, studying the enclosed photograph.

'I believe it's on the sideboard over there.'

Ravenscroft rose from the table, picked up the lens and took the photograph over to the window. 'Good lord!'

'Whatever is it, my dear?' asked a startled Lucy.

'I can see it now! This man in the photograph; I can see the resemblance now — the same eyes, nose and mouth. Good heavens! I would never have guessed it. Thomas Temple has been here all the time!'

Epilogue

As he took the locket from Ravenscroft's outstretched hand, tears began to form in the man's eyes.

'You must forgive me, Mr Ravenscroft, but I never expected to see this again. How did you come by it?'

'The dead man, Jacob, had it concealed amongst his private effects,' replied Ravenscroft.

'I am sorry, but you say Jacob is dead?'

'He was the dead man found hanging from a tree on Hangman Hill several weeks ago.'

'Yes, I recall reading about the incident in the local paper, but the report did not name the victim.'

'At that time we hadn't been able to identify the body. I'm pleased to say that his killers have now been apprehended.'

'But why would anyone want to have killed Jacob?'

'It's rather a long story, but it seems that he may have been involved in Lizzie Warren's death on Hangman Hill ten years ago, before he went to America. His killers evidently concluded that Jacob had killed Lizzie, and when they saw that he had returned to Hereford they took the law into their own hands.'

'This lady in the locket, I always knew that she was my mother. I say that because when I was growing up at the Foundling Hospital in London, I always believed that I had been given away by someone who must have once cared a great deal for me; and as I was growing up I imagined this beautiful woman who one day would come back and claim me. Then when I left the hospital at the age of sixteen, they gave me the locket, saying that its owner had been a gentlelady from Herefordshire. That was all they would say; and as I lay in my bed at night during the coming years, I would take out the locket, and open it, and place it on the pillow by the side of my head, and look at those features and know that she had once loved me, and that something terrible must have happened shortly after my birth that compelled her to give me up.'

'She was a single woman. The scandal would have destroyed both her and her family,' said Ravenscroft quietly.

'I was employed as a junior clerk at Mincing and Stricket in London, and one day they learnt that their agent in New York had been killed in some public house brawl, and they asked if I would like to take on the position,' continued the man with his narrative. 'As I was keen to see the world at this time, I readily accepted, but the position was not as I had imagined it. Their warehouse was situated in a not very attractive area of the city, and I was compelled to live out a lonely existence at Ma Scrivens' Lodging House in Manhattan. Then one day the police authorities raided the building where I worked and found some stolen items amongst our goods, and I was arrested. I was entirely innocent of the crime — you must believe me, Mr Ravenscroft; but although I pleaded my case, I was found guilty and sentenced to three years' imprisonment on Blackwell's Island. Often in my cell I would take out that locket and look at that face, and I promised myself that one day when I was free I would return to England and find my mother.'

'I understand that you shared a cell with Jacob. Did he ever tell you about why he'd been forced to leave England?' asked Ravenscroft.

'No; he told me nothing of his past life. Jacob was only in my cell for a few weeks, then he was released; and once he was gone I made the terrible discovery that he'd somehow appropriated the locket. Imagine my anguish, Inspector. The one possession that I valued above even my own life had been taken from me! I was distraught, but I still had the memories; and when I closed my eyes I could still see her face, and that gave me the strength to go on.'

'How did you gain employment at Macy's?'

'Because I had received a good education at the Foundling Hospital, I was able to put that to good use in helping a number of the inmates to read and write. The warden learnt of my industry, thought that I should be given a fresh start in life, and said he would do all that he could to help me secure honest employment upon my release. One of his friends was a partner in Macy's, and that is how I went to work at the department store. It was like a palace to me, and after all the drab unhappy years of loneliness it seemed almost like home working there.

'For a while I was happy, but all the time I was there I thought of nothing but England, and of my mother. Eventually I had saved enough money for the return passage to Liverpool. I didn't know where my mother lived, but the Foundling Hospital said she had come from Herefordshire, and so I came here, where I was fortunate to gain employment. I thought it expedient to change my name. I wanted to put the past behind me; it was to be a new beginning. My work has brought me a great deal of satisfaction over the years, Mr Ravenscroft, but I have always lived with the hope that one day I would see my mother again and that we would be united.'

'I have to tell you that your mother has never forgotten you, and like you has thought constantly that one day you will be together,' said Ravenscroft once the man had finished his account.

'And this is the house where she lives?' asked the man as the trap pulled up on the road outside The Verzons. 'It's a fine building.'

'Miss Constantine lives here with her brother,' said Crabb, bringing the horse to a standstill.

'Thank you, Mr Ravenscroft,' said the man, stepping down from the trap. 'Will you come with me? I'm sure that my mother would wish to express her gratitude to you in person.'

'I've taken the liberty of sending her a telegram this morning. She'll be expecting you. I think I won't intrude at this time. I wish you well,' said Ravenscroft with a smile.

'Thank you once again, Inspector.'

Ravenscroft and Crabb watched as Ronald Clifford, the Malvern librarian, opened the gates to The Verzons, and with one last wave disappeared from view.

'So, a satisfactory end to the case, would you not say so, Tom?' said Ravenscroft.

'Most satisfactory, sir,' replied Crabb, urging the horse forward.

'To think that I went halfway round the world looking for Maria Constantine's son, and all the time he was living not eight miles from Ledbury.'

'It is a strange world, sir.'

'Oh, Tom, I nearly forgot — this letter arrived for you this morning. Give me the reins while you look at it,' said Ravenscroft, removing an envelope from his inside coat pocket and passing it over with a broad smile to his constable. 'I had a word with the superintendent before I left for America.'

'A letter for me? It looks very formal,' said Crabb hesitantly.

'I think you'll be pleased when you read its contents.'

Crabb tore open the envelope and read the lines before exclaiming, 'My word, sir! I don't believe it. I don't deserve this.'

'You most certainly do. Congratulations, Detective Sergeant Thomas Crabb — upon a richly deserved promotion!'

We do hope that you have enjoyed reading this large print book.

Did you know that all of our titles are available for purchase?

We publish a wide range of high quality large print books including:
**Romances, Mysteries, Classics
General Fiction
Non Fiction and Westerns**

Special interest titles available in large print are:
**The Little Oxford Dictionary
Music Book
Song Book
Hymn Book
Service Book**

Also available from us courtesy of Oxford University Press:
**Young Readers' Dictionary
(large print edition)
Young Readers' Thesaurus
(large print edition)**

For further information or a free brochure, please contact us at:
**Ulverscroft Large Print Books Ltd.,
The Green, Bradgate Road, Anstey,
Leicester, LE7 7FU, England.
Tel:** (00 44) 0116 236 4325
Fax: (00 44) 0116 234 0205

Other titles published by Ulverscroft:

THE PERSHORE POISONERS

Kerry Tombs

1890: In the Worcestershire market town of Pershore, at Talbots' Lodging House, a recently arrived guest dies in mysterious circumstances. Detective Inspector Samuel Ravenscroft and his colleague, Constable Tom Crabb, are called in to investigate, and are presented with accusations that the dead man was poisoned — a theory borne out by circumstantial evidence. Then a second guest is killed: arsenic is suspected in both deaths, and the policemen's enquiries begin to unearth long-buried secrets. Meanwhile, an old case from Ravenscroft's past threatens to cast a shadow over the present . . .

THE DROITWICH DECEIVERS

Kerry Tombs

April 1890. Whilst visiting a local churchyard, the nine-year-old daughter of a prominent Droitwich businessman disappears without a trace. Detective Inspector Ravenscroft and his colleague, Constable Tom Crabb, investigate. Then, in a seemingly unconnected incident, Ravenscroft's wife, Lucy, is asked by a distraught mother to find the baby that she'd been compelled to give away. As the investigations proceed, both Ravenscroft and Lucy encounter the darkened world of Victorian child exploitation: lies, deceit and murder are commonplace — and they are stuck in a desperate race against time to save the endangered children . . .